CAN'T

When an American wallflower learns her younger sister is forbidden to become betrothed until someone courts her, she pays a duke to pretend to be her suitor.

Lucy Banks will never be mistaken for the belle of the ball. Her red hair, freckles, and reputation for surliness make that impossible, no matter how many coffers of coin her father procured on Wall Street. Unfortunately, her parents didn't move across the Atlantic so Lucy could struggle to find a husband. Even more unfortunately, her younger sister cannot have a suitor until Lucy's future is secure. Unless Lucy can find someone to court her, she is standing in the way of her sister's happiness. Fortunately, Lucy is willing to pay.

Harrison James, Duke of Sturbridge, might be beloved by the *ton*, but he has no intentions of ever marrying. That would mean exposing a bride to his secret, and that is impossible.

When Miss Banks offers him money to feign romantic interest in her, he reluctantly agrees. Once Lucy returns to New York, he can pronounce himself brokenhearted and avoid another year of questions. Lucy and the duke now only have one problem: they must not confuse their hearts with their fake courtship.

OTHER BOOKS IN *The Duke Hunters Club:*
  All You Need is a Duke
  My Favorite Duke
  A Duke Never Forgets
  The Duke Before Christmas

The Duke Meets His Matchmaker
The Truth about Princesses and Dukes
Can't Buy Me a Duke

CHAPTER ONE

"LUCY ALICE BANKS," Mama's voice barreled through their Grosvenor Square townhouse, evidently unperturbed by the abundance of thick marble and the presence of startled servants. "Get down here! At once!"

Lucy scurried from her room. Mama, Papa, and Isabella stood in the foyer. The crystals from the chandelier above made their clothes glimmer, an unnecessary addition to the shimmery overlay over Mama's and Isabella's gowns and their jeweled necklaces.

Both of Mama's arms had settled on her waist, and she glared with a ferocity soldiers might envy when seeking to intimidate their well-armed enemy. "You were reading."

"I—"

"Your dress is creased. You must have sat down after Rose prepared you."

"I'm sorry, I—"

"Never mind." Mama flung a pelisse at her. "Put this on. Let's hope Sir Seymour is stingy with his candles."

Lucy nodded dumbly and slipped the pelisse on. The ivory spotted fox trim was unnecessary in the warm June weather.

Mama had chosen it more for its vast expense than its practicality.

The butler opened the main door and shot Lucy a sympathetic look. No doubt, all the servants had heard Mama's increasingly frantic tirades on the importance of appearing immaculate, exuding femininity and charming a man into marriage. Unfortunately, Lucy hadn't succeeded at any of those tasks, particularly the latter and most important.

Mama and Papa hurried toward the coach. Isabella moved briskly after them, striding easily despite her stays and the need to ensure her hem remained mud-free. They scrambled inside, then the coach jerked to a sudden start. The horses hurried toward Sir Seymour's townhouse.

Finally, the horses stopped before an austere townhouse. Golden light glowed from a set of large windows, and music streamed faintly toward them.

"We've arrived!" Mama lunged for the door handle and hurried from the coach. The others followed, though at a slightly slower pace than Mama.

The steps and pavement were devoid of chattering *ton* members, and Lucy's heart fell. Normally, there was a long queue entering any ball. Had everyone already entered?

Lucy followed her family up the steps and braced for the crush of people inside. She prepared herself for clashing scents of floral and musk, and the jostling of people as they moved into a too-small place and spent too long craning their heads toward the ceiling, declaring the artist of whatever celestial and cherub-swarming ceiling superior to Michelangelo and Titian. She almost felt the barely restrained glowers of swift-moving footmen.

A violin screeched, and after her family had changed into their dance slippers, they ventured into Sir Seymour's ballroom. The walls were the serene green commonly found in duck ponds, and the floors were dark wood. Footmen in old-fashioned pantaloons and wigs flanked the banquet table as if to guard it. None of them glowered and none of them moved swiftly.

Sir Seymour marched toward them, and his face reddened from the exertion, the color emphasized by his white hair. Mama exchanged glances with Papa, then approached the host.

"Are we early to the ball?" Mama asked.

"Early? No such thing as early!" Sir Seymour's eyebrows pushed together.

"I meant not many people are present," Mama amended.

"Ah, quite, quite," Sir Seymour said. "Only the best of the best come here."

Mama gave a pleased smile. She craned her neck toward the few guests mingling about the banquet table, but Mama's expression sobered. "I don't recognize anyone."

"Then I shall do the introductions," Sir Seymour said jovially. "I hunt with them in Yorkshire."

"Ah," Mama said.

Lucy scanned the ballroom for any acquaintants. The ballroom was mostly empty. A few elderly women huddled near the fireplace, while their even more elderly husbands tottered about the punch table. They had heavy white sideburns that seemed formed in the view of offering extra warmth on chilly northern days. A lone violinist played in one section of the ballroom, even though most hosts and hostesses made sure at least a string quartet was present. The violist did not make up for the lack of accompaniment with talent, and perhaps the advanced age of the guests was not the sole reason for the empty dance floor.

"It seems awfully sparse here," Mama said.

"Sparse? Nonsense!" Sir Seymour grumbled. "Exclusive. Highly exclusive."

A footman gave a muffled snort, and Sir Seymour glared.

The footman lowered his silver platter. "Would you care for a drink, my lord?"

Sir Seymour snatched an entire glass of brandy and downed it. He placed the empty tumbler back on the tray, and it clinked loudly. He then took another glass of brandy and grinned.

"There's some event at Almack's," Sir Seymour said. "Those blasted proprietesses consider themselves exclusive. Obviously, everyone is missing out."

"Oh," Mama said. "I didn't know about that event."

"Then I reckon you weren't invited."

Mama stiffened.

"I wasn't either." Sir Seymour grabbed a flute of champagne from a waiter and slurped it down. "Damned snobs."

"I thought all English were snobs," Papa observed drily.

"Oh, yes." Sir Seymour nodded rapidly. "But most English snobs aren't as disagreeable looking as the proprietresses of Almack's. Revolting group of women, that's what I say!"

"You told them that?" Papa asked.

Sir Seymour gave a toothy grin and nodded his head rapidly. "Banned for life, I am. Think of that! Me, a baron from the great county of Yorkshire." Sir Seymour leaned closer to

Lucy's family. "Yorkshire is the most wonderful county in all of Britain. Have you visited yet?"

"No."

Sir Seymour heaved a disappointed sigh. "Americans. So uncultured."

"We've visited Bath though," Mama said brightly. "And some of the countryside."

"Ha! Some of those buildings in Bath are ancient. Created by Romans. All distasteful. Bunch of Italians."

Mama's smile tightened, though she valiantly continued the conversation. "The Roman Baths are lovely. I do recommend it."

"But can you hunt there?" Sir Seymour pressed. "Can you shoot game? Do falcons and foxes roam about those limestone travesties?"

"Falcons don't roam," Lucy said.

Sir Seymour fixed his beady gaze on her. "I personally ascribe to the notion that women should be seen and not heard. Sometimes they shouldn't even be seen."

Lucy flinched.

Sir Seymour raked his gaze over Lucy's figure with obvious concentration as if to count every freckle and compare every curve to those found in artists' manuals.

Mama clutched hold of Lucy's elbow, then grabbed Isabella. "Come, girls."

Sir Seymour smirked as Mama marched them from the baron.

"That, young ladies, was an insult." Mama glanced back at Sir Seymour. "From that vile man. Utterly abhorrent."

Isabella's face remained calm. "No doubt, he misspoke."

Mama narrowed her eyes. "He intended it as an insult. Though, Isabella, I'm certain he didn't include you."

Isabella shot a worried glance at Lucy, and Lucy's heart tumbled.

Mama was correct. He hadn't meant Isabella. Isabella exuded perfection.

Every man loved Isabella's large, wide-set eyes, just as every man loved her silky hair. Gentlemen adored her heart-shaped face and were apt to suddenly muse about the beauty of cheekbones, even though Lucy was certain none of them had given much thought to cheekbones and their potential for beauty before meeting Isabella.

Everyone remarked on Isabella's beauty to Lucy since they were small girls, as if they were all bewildered that Lucy, who had so clearly turned out all wrong, was the sister of someone so striking.

Isabella's personality was similarly devoid of flaws. A writer of maudlin allegories could not have concocted someone of better character. Isabella was kind and sweet. She didn't possess an actual halo, but people swarmed about her all the same. It didn't take them long to discover her beauty, and they flocked to her, offering her their meager jokes and compliments as tribute.

Lucy was accustomed to men rapidly approaching Isabella and commenting on her beauty before shooting Lucy disgruntled, obviously disappointed glances. Lucy didn't resemble Isabella. Lucy's figure was too rounded, a fact even the most expensive fabrics and most advanced fashion cuts failed to mask. Isabella resembled a dainty doll. No amount of ribbons and flounces and puffed sleeves ever made her look ridiculous. She always appeared exquisite.

There'd been a time when the prospect of attending balls had excited Lucy. She'd even been excited about visiting England, but she soon learned London balls were no different than New York ones. Both involved sitting in the smoky sections of the ballroom, waiting in vain for someone to ask her to dance.

Mama glowered at Lucy. "You are humiliating me."

"I-I'm sorry, Mama." Lucy's voice trembled. Even though she wasn't particularly fond of the value everyone placed on being beautiful, she abhorred not attaining that trait.

"All that money on a French modiste," Mama wailed, throwing her hands up with such violence the diamond bracelets on her wrists created an angry clang. "You're wearing the height of fashion, and yet..."

"It doesn't matter," Lucy said mournfully.

Mama blinked abruptly. "We'll find you a husband."

"I don't want a husband." Lucy wrapped her arms together and pressed them against her chest.

A husband was just a man one had married. Considering the generally unsatisfying behavior of men, marriage lacked appeal.

Suddenly, the door to the ballroom opened, and half a dozen men entered. Unlike the men already at the ball, these men were decidedly on the correct side of thirty-five. They were tall with chiseled features that the flickering candlelight adored. They shot wide grins at everyone. Their skin was sunkissed, and they emanated health.

"More guests!" Mama clapped her hands. "The Duke of Sturbridge is here. Think of that."

"And Lord Benedict Brooke." Isabella's long eyelashes fluttered, and a dreamy expression drifted over Isabella's perfect features.

"Yes, yes," Mama said. "Though Lord Brooke is a viscount. Sturbridge is a duke. And that's quite the best thing to be. His mother lives next door to us."

"Yes, Mama." Isabella's gaze remained transfixed on Lord Brooke.

Lord Brooke had the same flaxen hair as Isabella, and the same bright blue eyes. His coiffure was immaculately curled, but he never displayed the arrogance of some of the fashionable men who spoke about Beau Brummel in the same wondrous manner physicists adopted when speaking about Sir Isaac Newton.

The men swaggered into the ballroom. Other women turned toward them, no doubt appreciating their broad chests and towering heights and clear skins.

"Oh, my!" Mama fanned herself vigorously, unconcerned with damaging the expensive lace. "Perhaps this *will* be an interesting ball, after all."

Lucy nodded reluctantly. For a moment, she'd almost hoped Mama would insist they leave, and Lucy could finish her book. Still, she hadn't looked forward to Mama's accompanying anguished statements.

"Once dear Lucy marries, I think the Duke of Sturbridge might be perfect for you, Isabella," Mama said.

"Truly?" Isabella scrunched her lips, even though she'd warned Lucy on occasion that lip scrunching might lead to unflattering lines. "He is rather roguish. People say he has no intention of ever marrying."

Mama shrugged nonchalantly. "Men can be persuaded to marry, especially men in need of heirs. The important thing is whether or not he has money."

Papa cleared his throat with such force that several elderly guests stared. Clearly, Papa's vocal capacity was not daunted by their decreasing auditory abilities.

Mama's cheeks pinkened. "Obviously, money isn't the *only* important thing. Some men have money *and* are tolerable."

"Tolerable?" Papa bit into a small artichoke tart.

"Suitable," Mama corrected impatiently.

Papa raised his eyebrows.

Mama's shoulders slumped, and the faux flowers sewn onto her dress seemed to swallow her. "Wonderful. Obviously, that's what I meant."

"Obviously," Papa repeated, then offered Mama a canapé.

"Anyway," Mama said. "The Duke of Sturbridge's suitability for Isabella does not matter. Lucy must marry first."

"Truly?" A mournful look crossed over Isabella's impeccable features. Isabella seldom appeared anything but content, and Lucy drew her eyebrows together.

"Naturally." Mama jutted out her chin, oblivious to Isabella's uncharacteristic frown. "I won't have you marrying first."

"You're our baby," Papa said fondly.

"And Lucy will never marry if Isabella marries first," Mama chattered merrily. "People are already suspicious of her age. It wouldn't do to have her also have an already married sister. What would people think!"

"But that won't mean she'll be a spinster forever," Isabella said.

Mama sighed, and a sorrowful expression sailed over her face. "But that's exactly what it will mean. Remember Aunt Dorinda? She's older than me. Once I married, she never did."

"Maybe she didn't desire marriage," Lucy said.

"And willingly stay with my parents her entire life?" Mama wrinkled her nose. "Sweetheart, they must somehow have formed a good impression on you, but no one would desire that fate."

"Your mother is absolutely correct." Papa had evidently recovered from Mama's unromantic proclamation that money was essential for prospective suitors to possess for the opportunity to demean his in-laws.

"You remind me of Aunt Dorinda." Mama smoothed a lock of Lucy's hair.

"If she'd been a redhead," Papa said.

Lucy stiffened. "My hair is auburn."

Mama and Papa exchanged sympathetic glances as if to commiserate that their children would make outrageous statements into adulthood.

"I warrant Lord Brooke wants to join us." Papa hastily changed the subject and waved a gloved hand toward the viscount.

Lord Brooke was indeed shooting frequent glances at them. The candlelight glowed over his golden locks, and his round, pleasant face made him resemble an overgrown cherub.

"May I dance with him?" Isabella pleaded.

"How do you know he wants to dance with you?" Mama asked.

Isabella bit her lip and was suddenly silent.

Lucy crinkled her brow, as if she were still being taught by her governess and was contemplating a particularly difficult mathematics problem. Was it possible her sister had somehow formed an . . . attachment? No, that was unlikely, despite Isabella's beauty. Surely, it was unlikely. Perhaps Isabella had opted to stay in London, staying with her friend Emmaline, while Lucy and her parents went to Bath, but that didn't mean Isabella had already found a potential husband.

A vague unease stomped through Lucy. Isabella was younger than Lucy. Had she already found love? On her own?

Was Lucy already Aunt Dorinda? Lucy suddenly felt even more frumpy and conscious of the wrinkles on her gown.

"Do smile, my dear. I won't have the men thinking you're grumpy," Mama continued, oblivious to the smirks of the other partygoers. "We New Yorkers already have terrible reputations here."

"I don't think smiling is necessary," Lucy said, but her heartbeat sped, and she pasted a too-wide smile on her face.

"Of course, it's necessary," Mama's voice was shrill.

"Now, fill your dance card," Papa said.

"They don't do dance cards here," Mama scolded him.

"That is a problem," Papa said.

Her parents squabbled, and Lucy wandered away, conscious of her lack of dance partners. At some point, balls had become tricky. They were filled with people conversing, but Lucy had to pretend she was happy being alone.

No wonder people extolled marriage. It must be nice to always have someone with whom to speak and dance. The musicians played quickly, unperturbed by their task of forming the perfect note on their stringed instrument and equally undaunted by the task of remaining in utter harmony with one another, despite the flurry of voices about the banquet table and stomping of feet on the dance floor. At least they had something to do.

The season had started a month ago, and once wide-eyed debutantes now glided about the room with smug superiority, confident in their ability to receive requests for dances and accustomed to a flurry of compliments. Last year Lucy had been in Bath, but now she was in London. She missed Bath's honey-colored townhouses and its abundance of hills that assured all the carriages drove slowly and revealed startling, beautiful images of the town and city. She despised London's flatness, even if the wide streets were convenient to carriages.

Heavens, Lucy even missed her home. She'd never considered herself much of a New Yorker, but this past month she'd missed the bustling city. The staid sophistication of Grosvenor Square felt constraining.

Lucy approached the refreshment table. She brushed past women wearing sleek ivory gowns. The gowns lacked the excessive adornment of the Parisian creations Mama had purchased for Lucy, and even though she was certain her gown was more expensive, she suddenly felt gauche.

Lucy picked up a crystal tumbler of punch. The coquelicot color of the liquid failed to incite excitement. The bobbing orange and strawberry slices were similarly invigorating, but she sipped it tentatively.

"It's that Banks girl." An alto voice sounded behind Lucy, and she stiffened. "The American. You heard about her."

"*Everyone's* heard about her," another, more high-pitched voice said.

Giggling sounded.

Lucy's heartbeat quickened.

They were speaking about her. Lucy quelled her instinct to rush from the ballroom, handkerchief in hand. It was tempting to pretend she'd lost her hearing and simply smile placidly like some of the Greek statues that dotted the room. Perhaps that option was ineffective, lest these people decide to test her hearing capabilities, speaking louder in a narrower distance while also escalating the vileness of their comments.

Lucy swung around. Some of her punch *may* have slid from her crystal tumbler, and some of it *may* have spilled onto her dress, which unfortunately, most definitely, was a pale pastel yellow.

Two women giggled, not bothering to cover their mouths with their elaborate oriental fans.

Lucy recognized them: Lady Letitia and Miss Aurora Fairbanks.

The two women stared at her. Their cheeks didn't redden with embarrassment, and Lucy's throat dried.

Lady Letitia's thin eyebrows arched up. "My dear, you've ruined your dress."

"She's already ruined her reputation," Miss Aurora Fairbanks whispered at a volume she must know Lucy was certain to still hear.

Lady Letitia giggled and flapped her fan.

Lucy hurried away.

CHAPTER TWO

Most places were improvements on Almack's, but Sir Seymour's ball was one of the few exceptions. Harrison James, Duke of Sturbridge, cast a disgruntled look around the murky green ballroom. A few older women huddled by the fireplace while some other guests lingered near the punch table.

Everyone gawked at him. Harrison favored *not* being the center of attention. Unfortunately, that was exactly what he was.

He forced a smile on his face, even though the violin arrangement was hardly smile-inducing. "Do you want to stay?"

Benedict's eyes shimmered and shone, as if he'd entered a cathedral after a lengthy days-long pilgrimage on his knees. "Yes."

Harrison's stomach fell with a rapidity suited for a desire to disappear beneath the polished floorboards. He knew that look. That look had appeared on the faces of his best friends before they'd announced an inclination to marry and move to the countryside. When he'd seen his friends again, they'd been accompanied by spouses at whom they gazed cow-eyed. The other portion of the time had been spent loudly proclaiming their spouses' virtues and unparalleled beauty.

A dull ache slithered through Harrison's chest. "Who's the woman?"

"Miss Banks," Benedict said dreamily. His lengthy lashes fluttered, actually fluttered, and his cheeks were rosier than before.

Harrison blinked. "Miss Banks?"

He knew Miss Banks.

Other men had spoken about Miss Banks in his presence, but the discussion had hardly been flattering.

Harrison's nose wrinkled, and his eyebrows coursed up. "She's the target of your amorous impulses?"

Benedict's always amiable face stiffened. "You needn't contort your face so vilely. Miss Banks is an angel. A goddess. A—" Benedict stopped, perhaps flummoxed by what could surpass a goddess and valiantly sucked in a deep breath of air. "A most magnificent creature. No poet could conjure a more lovely being."

"Miss Banks?" Harrison repeated, and his eyebrows scrambled toward each other, as if to confer over the conundrum. "She's cantankerous."

Understanding flitted over Benedict's face, and he gave a compassionate smile. "You haven't met her."

"I have!" Harrison insisted. "The experience was . . . memorable."

The last statement was the politest thing he could say about Miss Banks. Most women didn't have bright red hair and American accents. They also didn't spend their time huffing and rolling their eyes.

"I am referring to Miss *Isabella* Banks." Benedict's eyes had that dreadful dewy sheen again.

Oh.

Evidently, that was the woman's sister.

"I haven't made her acquaintance," Harrison admitted.

Still, he doubted a younger version of Miss Banks would be an improvement. A younger version would simply have *more* energy. He didn't want to contemplate her powers of scowling.

"I'll introduce you," Benedict said with a beatific smile. He then sobered. "Though you mustn't steal her from me."

"I won't," Harrison said. "I have no intention of ever marrying."

Benedict snorted. "That is a most uncharacteristic statement from a duke."

Harrison chuckled, but the laughter was forced. "Let's meet your Miss Banks. I'll be a perfect gentleman, I promise."

An uneasy look drifted over Benedict's face. "You needn't be *too* perfect."

Harrison raised his eyebrows.

"I want her for myself," Benedict explained.

"Any woman would adore you," Harrison said, even though it felt odd to remind his friend of his advantages. Insecurity was not a common affliction for Benedict.

After all, Benedict was Lord Brooke. He was a viscount. And unlike most viscounts, he was young and handsome. He didn't even spend his time installing opera singers in expensive apartments and gambling at gaming hells.

No, Harrison was certain any woman would leap at the chance to become Lady Brooke and mistress of Elm Manor.

"You're besotted," Harrison said.

Benedict didn't attempt to deny Harrison's words. Instead, he batted his lashes again, and Harrison had the horrible sense his best friend had just moaned.

"When is the wedding?" Harrison teased.

Benedict's face sobered. "Miss Isabella Banks is not allowed to marry."

Harrison's lips twitched. "I'm certain an exception could be made for you."

"No." Benedict averted his eyes, and a mournful expression, suitable to reading the more serious sections of broadsheets, crossed over his face.

Blast.

Benedict was actually upset. Miss Isabella Banks wasn't allowed to marry.

Harrison furrowed his brow. "Isn't the whole point of bringing young ladies to this ball to have men propose to them? So, they'll be taken care of the rest of their lives?"

"Her parents insist her oldest sister becomes engaged first." Benedict's expression resembled that of a distraught peasant eying an invading army.

Harrison's chest tightened. They were waiting for Lucy Banks to marry? No man would ever do that. He shook his head. "I'm sorry, old chap."

"It is a hopeless desire."

"Perhaps her parents can be persuaded . . ."

Benedict shook his head.

"How terrible." Perhaps Harrison had no desire to marry, but he couldn't imagine being in love and thwarted.

Benedict lifted his chin in a brave manner. "Perhaps someone will marry Isabella's sister."

"Perhaps," Harrison said. "There's always hope."

Personally, he felt sorry for whichever poor sod ended up with Miss Lucy Banks.

Benedict nodded solemnly, but his face seemed stiffer than normal, and his eyes had a distinct dewy glint. "Indeed."

Damnation.

Benedict was upset.

"Well, why don't you at least introduce us?" Harrison suggested.

"Very well," Benedict said, and Harrison followed his friend to the other side of the ballroom.

Miss Lucy Banks's presence was immediately evident. Her red hair might as well be a beacon. She looked no more fashionable than she in the past. In fact, even her dress was wrinkled tonight, and red and orange splotches marred the yellow fabric. Clearly, she noticed him, for she glared.

"Are you certain Miss Isabella Banks is different from her sister?" Harrison asked.

"Most different," Benedict said in that same dreamy, awestruck voice.

Mr. and Mrs. Banks parted, and a blonde woman who could only be Miss Isabella Banks appeared. Benedict was right. She looked nothing like her older sister. Her hair was a pale flaxen color, and her large, wide-set eyes were a bright blue that no doubt compelled suitors to immediately rhapsodize about the wonders of the ocean. Her figure was slim, though not to such a degree that she could be labeled skinny. She simply resembled a Greek goddess.

Her eyes lit up immediately when she saw Benedict, and Harrison's heart warmed. Even though he grumbled about his friends marrying, given the fact he would never partake in that particular institution, he enjoyed seeing his friend so happy.

"Your Grace!" Mrs. Banks sank into a deep curtsy.

Her husband looked at her askance, as if wondering whether he should assist her up.

"Bow, Mr. Banks," Mrs. Banks ordered in a loud whisper. "Bow."

With obvious reluctance, Mr. Banks bowed. "Your Grace."

Harrison and Benedict also bowed, murmuring various pleasantries.

"You remember my daughter?" Mrs. Banks pointed at Lucy.

Lucy observed him sullenly from half-closed eyes.

"Yes," Harrison said promptly. "She is unforgettable."

Mr. Banks smiled, but Lucy seemed to be experimenting to see whether she could transform her eyes into daggers. No one had ever glowered at him with such intensity.

He turned to Mrs. Banks. "I—er—have not met your other daughter, though."

"I suppose I can introduce you," Mrs. Banks said reluctantly.

Harrison exchanged glances with Benedict. Clearly, Mrs. Banks was as protective of her younger daughter as people said.

"Your Grace, this is Miss Isabella Banks." Mrs. Banks gestured to the blonde woman beside her. "Isabella, this is the Duke of Sturbridge."

Harrison lowered his torso. "A great pleasure to make your acquaintance."

Miss Isabella Banks smiled, and even though Harrison's heart didn't adopt a dangerous pace, he understood why people would be taken with her. She resembled a real-life doll. In addition to her wide-set eyes, she had rosebud lips, and her blonde hair was arranged in perfect ringlets. She wouldn't look out of place in a toy shop.

"You probably want to dance with my sister," Lucy said grouchily.

Her mother shot her a horrified glance. "You mustn't say that."

"It's true, isn't it?" Lucy asked stubbornly.

The corners of Harrison's lips twitched. He shot a glance at Benedict. His friend's face had turned white, and tension emanated from him. The man was smitten.

"Actually, Miss Banks," Harrison said, "I had hoped to dance with you."

"Me?" Lucy's eyes widened. He'd never noticed they were emerald before, but now it seemed impossible to ignore. Pity such pretty eyes had been wasted on such a person of such disagreeableness.

"Indeed," Harrison said, conscious of Benedict's shoulders lowering.

"And I would like to dance with you," Benedict said hastily to Lucy's sister.

She gave a pretty smile and accompanied the viscount onto the dance floor.

"Miss Banks?" Harrison repeated.

"She says yes!" her mother squealed. "She says yes."

Harrison gazed warily about the ballroom. That volume of voice was normally reserved for when daughters received proposals from their suitors.

Most of the ballroom stared, evidently more intrigued by his exchange with the Banks family than the prospect of bouncing up and down to the imperfectly played violin.

"She's going to dance with me," he mouthed to the biggest gossip. "Nothing more."

People gave an understanding nod.

Reluctantly, Miss Lucy Banks took his hand. An odd shiver moved through him as if something momentous had happened.

But then, of course, something momentous *had* happened. He was going to dance with the most undesirable woman in the room. She had a miserable look on her face.

"I promise not to step on your toes," he said.

"I'll throttle you if you do."

He chuckled despite himself. After all, he didn't need to look like he was having a good time. He just needed to dance with her, so Benedict could dance with her sister.

"Dancing with me isn't a miserable prospect," he said.

She raised an eyebrow.

"That's not a controversial statement," he insisted.

"Do you begin all your dances by saying that?"

"Only with you," he said lightly.

She smiled, though he wasn't certain whether it was because they were joining the other dancers and she would no longer be forced into prolonged conversation with him.

The music began, and Harrison moved. Thankfully, the musicians had decided on a reel and not a waltz. Holding Miss Banks in his arms was the absolute last thing Harrison desired. Hopefully, he would not encounter her after tonight.

CHAPTER THREE

"Wake up!"

Lucy rubbed her eyes, then stared at a slender figure beside her bed. "Isabella?"

"Yes," Isabella whispered impatiently. "Get up!"

Lucy scrambled up. Even though it was summer, and it was almost always light when Lucy awakened, today darkness shrouded the room. "Did something happen? Mama? Papa?"

"They're fine. They're sleeping."

"Oh." Lucy furrowed her brow and glanced at the cover. Snuggling back into bed seemed exceedingly tempting.

Isabella marched to the drapes and opened them. "You need to dress."

Moonlight floated into the room, casting a magical glow over all the furniture.

"It's the middle of the night," Lucy said.

"No, it's *almost* morning," Isabella corrected. "The sun will rise in half an hour."

"What does that have to do with me?"

"Then we will be out, enjoying it," Isabella said.

Lucy stared at her younger sister. "You're suggesting we leave the townhouse?"

Isabella nodded impatiently.

"But we can't do that."

They couldn't leave the townhouse. Not alone. Not without Mama.

"Rose will join us," Isabella said. "Besides, we'll be chaperoning each other."

"I see," Lucy said uncertainly.

"*And* it will be light soon."

"Where will we go?" Lucy asked.

Isabella gave a mysterious smile, and Lucy suddenly felt sorry for Mona Lisa's sister.

Lucy sighed and rose. "I suppose I could dress."

Isabella opened Lucy's wardrobe. "You don't wear enough pink."

"Because I despise the color."

Isabella flung Lucy's only pink gown onto the bed. "Pink enhances your complexion."

Personally, Lucy didn't think making her face appear redder was a vital component for looking presentable. Still, she allowed Isabella to help her into the dress.

"Mama won't like this," Lucy said.

"After today, Mama will be ecstatic."

"Indeed?"

Isabella's smile faltered. "Though it's not necessary to tell her straight away. Will you

join me?"

"Naturally." Lucy hadn't expected her perfect sister to rebel, but she wouldn't protest, even if the whole thing was terribly unconventional.

"Thank you." Isabella rang the bell pull, and Rose arrived shortly.

"You're up!" Rose's eyes were wide.

Isabella jutted out her chest. "I dressed her myself."

Rose scrutinized the various buttons on Lucy's dress. "Excellent, miss."

"I helped," Lucy said.

"Splendid," Rose said uncertainly, perhaps wondering why she'd been called.

"Rose, we're going to go outside," Isabella said. "You are to accompany us."

Rose bit her lower lip and twirled a dark ringlet of hair in a nervous manner. "You're not normally awake at this time."

"But we are today," Isabella said. "It would be a shame to miss the early morning."

"I should ask your mother."

"And wake her?" Isabella scoffed. "I doubt she would appreciate that."

"I—er—suppose not," Rose said miserably. "You wouldn't prefer to wait?"

"Naturally not."

Lucy stared at her younger sister. When had Isabella gained such confidence? It wasn't unwelcome, but confusion coursed through Lucy.

Soon Isabella, Rose, and Lucy strode through the townhouse and exited onto Grosvenor Square. It was so early, even the butler had not taken his customary position by the door, and they did not encounter any servants.

An icy breeze assailed them, and Lucy wrapped her arms underneath her cloak.

"Are you going to tell us where we're going now?"

"She's walking in the direction of Hyde Park," Rose said.

Date 9-19-25

M

Address

Reg. No.	Clerk	Account Forward		
1			3	00
2				
3	C.C.			
4				
5				
6				
7				
8				
9				
10				
11				
12				
13				
14				
15			3	00

A-1200/3510/3530
T-45202/46202/46203

Your Account Stated to Date - If Error is Found, Return at Once

Thank You
Call Again

We appreciate your patronage
and hope we may continue to merit it
If we please you, tell your friends.
If we don't, tell us.
We strive to satisfy.

Indeed, Isabella *was* marching west on Upper Brook Street. Unless they had a neighbor whom Isabella adamantly wanted to visit, they would be there soon.

The sun rose, and long pink and tangerine sunbeams played over the otherwise proper and staid houses.

Isabella spread her hands out triumphantly. "Isn't it beautiful?"

"Yes," Lucy said as they crossed the street to enter the park.

Hyde Park had seemed jarring amidst the rows of carefully designed townhouses, complete with elaborate facades. Sunlight danced amongst the soaring trees that lined the groomed paths, lending the park an ethereal aura. They might as well be hundreds of miles removed from London and its normal bustle. Huge, thick trees stretched out their lofty branches, adorned with chestnuts, at regular intervals. A fresh scent wafted about her, and for a moment, it didn't matter they were sneaking into the park early in the morning. It only mattered they were here.

"We're in a hurry." Isabella lengthened her strides and jutted her chin in the confident manner prevalent in merchants assured of their good fortune.

Lucy scampered after her. "Are you meeting someone?"

"We're visiting the Serpentine," Isabella said.

"Indeed?" Lucy had visited the Serpentine before. Visiting it again hardly required such subterfuge.

"The men are at the Serpentine," Isabella explained.

"You mean for us to watch the rowing?" Rose asked, and Lucy widened her eyes.

"Yes." Isabella gave a serene smile, as if she had not just dragged them out to watch aristocratic men exercise.

IT WAS NOT RESPECTABLE.

Lucy was certain about that.

Watching men exercise must be one of the least respectable activities one could do.

Isabella unfolded a thin blanket and laid it on a grassy spot that overlooked the Serpentine.

Various dukes and earls, viscounts and barons, stripped off their tailcoats. They stretched, showcasing the muscular girth beneath their shirts. Some pushed themselves back and forth off the ground, emphasizing their forearms' capability for strength, while others squatted. Lucy removed her gaze from rounded bottoms and broad shoulders.

"We shouldn't be here," Lucy said miserably.

"Nonsense," Isabella said. "It is imperative you find a husband."

"That doesn't mean we have to watch strange men exercise."

Isabella arched an eyebrow. "First of all, they're not strange. They're titled lords."

"All?" Rose gasped and jerked her head toward them.

"They're handsome, are they not?" Isabella asked.

Lucy chose not to answer that question.

The men piled into a long rowing boat, evidently eager to traverse the Serpentine.

"Besides, it is a fact universally acknowledged that men are lazy creatures."

Rose stared at the boat as it moved over the Serpentine at a brisk clip. "They don't appear lazy."

"No." Lucy followed her gaze, conscious of the synchronized movements of the men as they wielded oars in perfect unison. The boat moved rapidly.

"I wasn't referring to their inclination for physical activity," Isabella said. "Men are prone to marrying someone whom they see often. Familiarity makes the heart grow warmer."

"I thought familiarity breeds contempt," Lucy said. "And that distance makes the heart grow fonder."

Isabella waved her hand dismissively. "Perhaps the saying is not of the utmost importance."

"Is there a particular reason why I must find a husband?" Lucy's voice wobbled despite her best efforts.

Isabella's face sobered, and she took Lucy's hands in her own. "Benedict proposed while we were dancing last night."

Lucy straightened. "Indeed? You didn't say anything!"

"You'll be a viscountess." A joyful smile leaped onto Rose's round face, and she clapped her hands.

"Ideally." Isabella's lips remained drawn into a tight line.

"Our parents won't let you marry," Lucy said faintly.

Isabella nodded.

"But he's a viscount!" Rose exclaimed. "And so charming."

Isabella's eyes appeared sorrowful, but she nodded. "He is."

"Our parents will want me to marry first," Lucy explained.

"Or at least be courting someone," Isabella said.

Lucy bit her lip.

"You must find a suitor." Isabella leaned toward her and an odd determination caused her chin to jut out. Her cerulean eyes were transformed to steel.

Lucy crossed her arms automatically.

Isabella's eyes dropped to Lucy's arms, and she shrugged. "Unless you want to doom us to a lifetime of remaining with our parents."

Lucy shuddered. Permanent spinsterhood was an unwelcome thought. Being considered one now sufficed in dreadfulness.

"I'm not that old," Lucy protested.

Isabella's eyebrows lurched upward. "You're twenty-three."

Lucy grimaced. "You needn't say that so loudly."

Lucy had gone to a fancy finishing school in Boston, and she'd been marched before all the eligible men in New York. Unfortunately, those men had been wary of her. Or at least, she'd thought they'd been wary.

Papa's millions were impressive on a ledger, but everyone knew Papa had once been poor. When everyone in New York's upper crust longed to be viewed as the equals to London's *ton*, that was scarcely forgivable. Mama had ushered Lucy to the continent in order to find an aristocrat appreciative of a sizeable dowry who might not know Papa's unvarnished origins.

Perhaps if Isabella had attended the balls instead of Lucy, Isabella might have been whisked away by some New Yorker with no trouble at all. Perhaps Papa's one-time poverty was not the problem. Perhaps the problem was simply Lucy. She was too brash, too open with her emotions, and not pretty enough to counter her disadvantages.

"I'm trying to help you," Isabella reminded her.

Lucy's stomach turned miserably. "I know."

Everyone sought to help her. Her parents were even trying to help her. What other parents would move across the ocean to Grosvenor Square, the most fashionable and expensive square in all of Europe?

Lucy raked her hand through her hair. A strand fell, and Lucy attempted to tuck it back into her chignon. "It's not easy."

Isabella crossed her arms. "I managed to find someone."

Lucy shifted her legs over the grass. "And that's—er—wonderful."

But Isabella was different from her. Isabella was elegant and alluring. Lucy had spent her life hearing other people exclaim about Isabella's beauty, expressing relief Isabella did not share Lucy's hair color.

No. Isabella's triumph on the marriage mart couldn't be replicated by Lucy. She knew that, even if Isabella didn't understand. Isabella had always dazzled everyone. She didn't know what life was like when one was not. Isabella hadn't experienced disappointed sighs upon entering a room.

Isabella's eyes brightened, perhaps imagining Lucy marrying, unaware she was contemplating the impossible.

"You know Mama and Papa want you to marry first. Having an unmarried older sister is embarrassing."

"Isabella!" Lucy said in an outraged tone.

"Well, it is," Isabella said staunchly, though her cheeks did pinken. Perhaps she regretted her frankness. "It's the sort of thing that might make the viscount wonder."

"Then he wouldn't deserve you." Lucy crossed her arms and returned her attention to the rapidly moving boat filled with appealing aristocrats. "Besides Lord Brooke won't change his mind. He's smitten."

Isabella ignored Lucy. "I think any of those men might make a good husband. Look how good-natured they are."

Lucy stared at the men.

They were cheerful and hardworking, clearly undaunted by the early hour.

"Everyone complains about matchmaking mamas," Lucy said. "They should be talking about matchmaking sisters."

Isabella's pink lips formed a smug smile. "We're a rarity. You'll find someone, I'm certain. He'll be as remarkable as the viscount."

Lucy wished that were true. "What do you suggest I do?"

"Just be where they can see you and look exquisite," Isabella said. "That always works for me."

Lucy tried not to roll her eyes. Lucy required a better plan.

CHAPTER FOUR

"One, two, three, row," Harrison's voice barreled through the crisp morning air, unmarred by raindrops or England's familiar blustery wind. "One, two, three, row!"

The boat moved swiftly over the Serpentine.

Strictly speaking, they weren't supposed to practice here. Still, there was no more beautiful place in England, and until one of the princes exited Kensington Palace and explicitly forbade them, Harrison would continue.

Hyde Park was empty. Later, smartly dressed women would promenade about the park, twirling parasols they didn't require, given the wide brims of their hats and the general absence of sun. Some men would bring their horses to Rotten Row, enjoying their elevated position, given the frequency of their smug smiles. But now, any man in possession of his own horse was doing the very best thing to do on a Saturday morning—sleeping.

No, this was Harrison's favored time to be in the park. Privacy was something to be prized, and not simply because of a certain secret.

Harrison's chest tightened, as it always did when he contemplated his childhood. That was behind him, though. No one would know. If someone would have discovered his secret, they would have done so long ago.

"One, two, three, row," Harrison hollered, his voice soaring over the oars splashing through the water. "One, two, three, row."

Something red distracted him. Red *hair*. Three young women sat on a blanket, evidently undaunted by the dew and the fact it was six in the morning. Nobody should be here at six in the morning, and certainly not young women.

He knew those women. He'd seen them last night. What on earth was Lucy Banks doing here? And Isabella's sister? No glittering jewels were draped upon their wrists and necks now, but it was unmistakable. They were the Banks sisters. He assumed the third woman was their maid.

He scowled.

"Sturbridge?" Sir Augustus Sloane asked.

Harrison sighed. No doubt Augustus was confused why he had stopped counting. It wasn't difficult to count to three, after all. Harrison should know how to do it. He practiced every morning.

Augustus glanced toward the women. "You're distracted by those chits."

"I am not," Harrison said staunchly.

Augustus gave him an odd glance, and Harrison bit his lip. Perhaps it hadn't been necessary to be quite so opposed.

"Don't you think it's strange those women are there at this time?"

"Perhaps they enjoy the scenery."

"That corner is not particularly scenic."

"They are Americans. They may consider that corner scenic."

"There's nothing wrong with those women," Benedict pouted. "One of them is Aphrodite herself."

"Not the other one," Augustus grumbled.

Harrison frowned.

"She has red hair," Augustus said. "It's an impossibility."

"Botticelli's Venus has red hair," Harrison said, oddly perturbed at Augustus.

"Botticelli was an Italian," Augustus said. "Strange creatures, Italians."

There was no retort for that.

"You're supposed to be rowing," Harrison said.

"Well, you're supposed to be counting," Augustus said.

Harrison glowered.

Augustus was right, but he was hardly going to tell him that.

"One, two, three, row," Harrison shouted.

No doubt, the women were here to observe Benedict. Harrison shouldn't be contemplating them. He shouldn't muse over what the bright sun did to Lucy's red hair and how it glimmered with extra force, and he shouldn't speculate what her skin might look like under the shimmering sunshine. Would it have a velvety sheen to it?

He should concentrate on rowing.

"One . . . two. . ." Harrison's voice trailed.

"You're off your game," Benedict said.

"I am not," Harrison said stoutly. "I'm never off my game."

"You're counting imperfectly," Benedict said.

"I said the numbers in the correct order."

"Not all the numbers," Benedict muttered.

Harrison glowered. "We've done sufficient rowing."

"Are you certain?" Benedict asked.

"Perhaps his arms are tired," Augustus said.

"My arms are never tired," Harrison said. "I'm just concerned for yours."

Augustus raised an eyebrow.

"And I need to visit my office," Harrison said. "I might have mail."

Augustus sighed. "Most people depend on their estate managers."

"I enjoy the work."

That much, at least, was true.

Augustus nodded to the others, and they rowed to the embankment.

"It is astounding you still let your mother live in your Grosvenor Square house," Benedict mused.

"She's always done that," Harrison replied.

"Yes, but you're the duke. You could host balls in your house with regularity."

"And sometimes she does host balls," Harrison said. "She's hosting one tonight."

"Yes." Benedict tilted his head and observed him. "I'm just saying you're an excellent son."

Harrison gave a tight smile. "I'll take that as a compliment."

"He's probably grateful his mother doesn't make him marry someone," Augustus said.

Benedict chuckled. "Oh yes, that probably is true."

"Perhaps Harrison bribed her not to indulge in her matchmaking instincts so she could continue to live there." Augustus's laughter strengthened like a carriage speeding over the Great North Road that could not be easily stopped, and more men joined.

Harrison rolled his eyes. "I don't like this discussion."

"Because it's true," one of the men said.

It was not true.

But he couldn't admit that to them. He couldn't let them suspect his secret.

Harrison raised his chin. "My mother isn't against me marrying. She simply understands I am reluctant."

"That is remarkably amiable of her," Augustus said. "I've never even seen your mother push you to dance with someone at a ball. Our mothers do that constantly."

"Your average matchmaking mama would win any wrestling match," Benedict observed.

"Perhaps your mother can start giving lessons on patience and restraint, all those values deacons discuss in church but are never implemented at home," Augustus continued. "At least, when future grandchildren are concerned."

Harrison gave a weak smile. "Truly, that hasn't come up. She's quite normal, I assure you."

Benedict scrutinized him. "Lucky bastard."

Something in his friend's gaze made Harrison shiver. It was suddenly important to change the conversation.

"Let's go speak with the women," Benedict said.

"Truly?" Harrison shot a nervous look at Lucy and her sister.

"There's not more wonderful company in all of London." Benedict strode toward the women, and his eyes shimmered.

"THEY'RE COMING," ISABELLA squealed. She clapped her hands and shot Lord Brooke a sultry come-hither look.

Lucy swallowed hard. Since when had her sister shot sultry looks at men?

Isabella glanced at her. "Remember to smile."

Right.

Lucy could smile. She'd moved her lips upward on many occasions.

Still, tension moved through her, and she stiffened.

The men swaggered toward them. Gone were their tailcoats and jeweled waistcoats. Their cravats were not tied with their customary flourish, and their wet shirts clung to their chests in interesting manners. Heavens, the muscular planes of their torsos were visible, and Lucy had an odd urge to contemplate what they might look like without their shirts.

"On second thought," Isabella said. "Perhaps you shouldn't smile."

Right.

That was even easier.

Normally, Lucy explained how things worked to Isabella. She was the older sister. But suddenly, she felt uneasy. Men were mysterious creatures, and she missed Bath and her friends. It was far easier to speak to them than to talk to a man. Would these men expect her to speak of athletic matches?

Lord Brooke was flanked by two men. Lord Augustus Sloane and the Duke of Sturbridge. The duke strode toward them. His face had a grim expression, one she associated with people on the verge of doing unpleasant activities, such as walking a plank, and he veered away and marched toward the edge the park.

Her heart tumbled.

The man had seemed happy on the boat, at least until he saw them. She smoothed her dress, preferring to focus on alleviating creases than on observing the men.

"Lord Brooke. We meet again." Isabella waved.

"What an unexpected surprise," Lord Brooke said.

Isabella giggled, and Lucy jerked her head toward her sister. Had Isabella and Lord Brooke planned this?

But of course, they had. They'd danced together last night. Lucy eyed her sister's suitor skeptically. Surely, he shouldn't be encouraging her sister to do things that could get her into trouble? The walk to Hyde Park from Grosvenor Square was safe, but it had been early in the morning. If someone had accosted them, few people would have been present to be of assistance.

"How nice to see you again, Miss Banks," Lord Brooke said to her.

"Er—yes." Her voice was gruff, and she *may* have been glaring.

Lord Brooke's face lost its earlier composure. "Isn't it a magnificent day?"

"I suppose," Lucy grumbled. "I imagine the day will be even nicer later when the sun has more chance to warm everything."

"Are you cold?" Concern emanated through Isabella's voice.

Lucy crossed her arms and glowered at Lord Brooke. "I'm fine."

"It was foolish of me to term the day magnificent," Lord Brooke said. "After all, how can any day be magnificent when compared to your sister?"

Lucy stiffened.

"Her eyes surpass the sky, and her smile is more marvelous than the sounds of the birds chirping."

"Are you certain her laugh isn't more wondrous than that of birds chirping?" Lucy grumbled.

Lord Brooke's eyes widened. "That too." He pressed his hand against his heart. "You do understand. Sturbridge called you cantankerous, but clearly, he was inaccurate."

Isabella cast a nervous glance at Lucy, then returned her gaze to Lord Brooke. "You shouldn't say that."

"Your sister understands," Lord Brooke said.

"Where did Sturbridge go?" Lucy asked, eager to change the conversation.

Lord Brooke sighed. "He was supposed to be here. He said he had to meet with his mother."

Sir Augustus rolled his gray eyes. "What mother is awake at this time?"

"I think he might suffer from shyness," Lord Brooke said. "I've never seen him attached to a woman."

"Never?" Lucy widened. "But he's so—"

"—Handsome?" Isabella prompted and smirked.

Both Lucy and Lord Brooke glowered, but Isabella's eyes only sparkled with more force.

"He's not *that* handsome," Lord Brooke said finally.

"Well, I personally am partial to blonds," Isabella said, and Lord Brooke's chest expanded.

Harrison had silky dark hair that tumbled over his brow in an alluring manner and matched his arresting solemn eyes.

Sir Augustus turned away. "I think I might pay a call to my mother."

"No!" Isabella and Lord Brooke exclaimed simultaneously. They stared at each other, then giggled.

"You must sit, Sir Augustus." Isabella gestured toward the blanket with a confident charm that equaled the most accomplished hostess in Mayfair. "There's a place beside my lovely sister."

Was this Lucy's potential husband? She glanced at him carefully. The man was handsome in a conventional manner, and no painter would struggle on how to depict him in a flattering manner. No doubt, it would be hard for Sir Sloane not to appear muscular if his chosen morning activity was rowing.

Sir Augustus sat down reluctantly. "Tell me, Miss Banks, how do you like London?"

"It's nice," Lucy said obediently, even though that adjective wasn't the precise one she would have used to describe it.

"Ah." Sir Augustus nodded as if she'd said something insightful.

"Have you followed the racing?" Sir Augustus asked hopefully.

"No," Lucy said flatly.

Disappointment drifted over Sir Augustus's square face.

"You must be happy to be out of New York," Sir Augustus remarked.

"Indeed?"

"Good to surround yourself with some culture," Sir Augustus continued. "See some paintings."

"I assure you we have paintings in New York."

Sir Augustus scrunched his lips together, as if to denote he found her statement highly questionable, but was too polite—no doubt, a quality he thought pertained solely to the English, to argue that point.

"You should visit New York sometime," Lucy said.

Sir Augustus widened his eyes, and his thin lashes fluttered back furiously. "Isn't that somewhat...forward of you?"

Drat.

Isabella frowned at her slightly and shook her head.

Obviously, Lucy hadn't wanted Sir Augustus to visit *her*, but from his priggish and self-satisfied expression, that was precisely what he thought. If only the grass could promptly propagate and enshroud her in its verdant blades.

Why was this so difficult?

"Not to see me obviously," Lucy said, and Isabella shot her an approving smile. "After all, I am in London, and you would be thousands of miles away."

That was a blissful thought, and she smiled.

Sir Augustus scowled. Perhaps he thought her rude to imply she would be happy if he were many miles away. Well, she didn't care. That would be an improvement.

Isabella sighed, perhaps reading her mind. "It's unfortunate Sturbridge had to depart."

"I think it's damned odd," Sir Augustus said. "He should be living in the townhouse or purchase another one. Duke shouldn't reside in clubs. I suppose it's a financial issue. Incomprehensible, the whole thing."

Lord Brooke shot Sir Augustus a warning look, and Isabella hastily remarked over the loveliness of the flowers.

The duke had financial difficulties. How unexpected. Lucy contemplated Sir Augustus's statement as Lord Brooke gallantly compared Isabella favorably to each and every flower in their vicinity. Evidently, Isabella's blue eyes surpassed the splendor of the bluebells, her elegance exceeded that of the peonies, and her poise outshone the orchids.

ONCE THEY RETURNED to their townhouse, Lucy paced her chamber. She required an idea. Any idea would do, provided it was brilliant.

She did not desire to stand between her sister and her sister's chance of finding happiness with a handsome, if somewhat dull, viscount.

Lucy needed to be courted and she needed her parents to be so convinced a betrothal was forthcoming that they would permit her sister to be wooed. It was the only way.

Isabella might consider it simple to find a man. Clearly, she thought all one had to do was to smile prettily into the middle distance and wait for some man to offer his undying affection and promise to take financial care of her for the rest of their lives.

Lucy knew it was not that easy. She was older than Isabella, and no man had ever approached her bearing compliments and declaring an intention to forever join their lives together in this world and the celestial one, even if suitors constantly sprung up around Isabella. A swarm of men always swooped around Isabella as if she were the light and they were, well, gnats.

Lucy sighed. If she couldn't find a man with actual amorous and marital intentions, she required a man willing to enter a faux relationship.

She tapped her hands against a sideboard and pondered.

This man naturally could not be seeking a wife. Such a thing was impossible. After all, the worst thing would be if she entered into an arrangement with him, and he promptly tumbled in love with someone else. If Isabella was correct, and it only took a glimpse at someone to tumble into love, then danger lurked everywhere. No, she needed a man who did not want a wife.

In other words, she needed a man like Harrison James, the Duke of Sturbridge.

After all, Benedict had told Isabella that Harrison was a perpetual bachelor. Moreover, even though he was a duke, he still stayed in the Robertson's Gentleman's Club. Perhaps most people weren't talking about the duke's evident poverty, but Sir Augustus had more than implied that the duke must be devoid of the overflowing coffers that so often accompanied vast estates. After all, why else would the duke stay in a Gentleman's Club?

At least Lucy possessed vast wealth. Papa's success on Wall Street was unrivaled. He didn't mind when Mama dragged them all to Paris to buy lavish gowns, then ushered them to London to display them in glittering ballrooms.

Lucy scrunched her lips together. She could pay the duke for his efforts. Perhaps that would be sufficient to overlook the inconvenience of being viewed as being smitten with her. Besides, the duke's best friend was Lord Brooke. The duke might be sentimentally inclined to assist for his friend's sake, if for nothing else.

Of course, the duke wasn't fond of her. She knew that. His eyes never gleamed when he saw her, despite the enthusiasm with which her mother had initially attempted to place them together.

Still, this was a business arrangement. Personal taste and sentiment had no place in any decisions.

Tonight there was a ball at Harrison's mother's house in Grosvenor Square. She would be able to tell the duke her plan. She would make it so appealing he could not refuse.

Lucy smiled, then walked to her wardrobe where she kept her gold coins and put them carefully into her reticule. Tonight would be marvelous.

"It is rather odd that a future duke wasn't sent to Eton or Harrow, isn't it?"

"Not that odd. It was my parents' decision."

"Surely they would have wanted you to meet other people. No one sends their children there purely for the education."

"I was a sickly child."

Augustus rolled his gaze over Harrison, and Harrison's skin prickled. "You don't *seem* sickly now."

"No," Harrison said shortly. "The convalescence was effective. I'm cured."

"Evidently."

Harrison raked his hand through his hair. "It's necessary to inspect the buffet table. I'm sorry, Augustus. Hosting duties and all that. All terribly dull."

No sooner had he approached the buffet table, then Miss Banks darted toward him, and his stomach fell. She crossed the ballroom with a speed more suited to brisk morning walks through Hyde Park, and her chin jutted forward in a decidedly resolute manner.

This was not good.

He'd seen that look of bold tenacity before. Normally, matchmaking mamas approached him with that doggedness, but he'd been suspicious of Miss Bank's appearance in Hyde Park. If she could waylay him in a park while he was exercising at an ungodly hour, he didn't want to contemplate what she might do here after spending the day consuming coffee.

Harrison coughed loudly, then turned to Sir Augustus. "Did I mention I wasn't feeling well?"

"No," Sir Augustus said flatly.

"Er—well, I am." Harrison rested a hand over his brow in what he hoped was a delicate manner. "Not feeling well, that is. Must be that childhood affliction. Give my—er—apologies to anyone who asks for me."

Sir Augustus scrutinized him. Harrison wondered whether his friend had ever considered becoming a magistrate. Clearly, he was in possession of the correct amount of natural suspicion.

"You're leaving?" Sir Augustus gazed at him dubiously. "Your own ball?"

"Yes," Harrison said, then hastened away.

THE NIGHT HAD BEEN disastrously uneventful. What duke left his own ball?

Lucy required a new plan—one where she could speak to him alone.

A thought occurred to her. Didn't the duke use the library at his mother's townhouse in Grosvenor Square? Perhaps she could find him there, then outline the wonderfulness of her plan in private. She could hardly march up the steps of the townhouse by herself, and this was hardly a conversation to be had in front of a chaperone, but what if she approached the library by the courtyard? Libraries were generally not placed on second or third stories, and if she could enter through a window...

Well, it was a thought. It was the best thought she had.

Lucy rapidly changed into the darkest afternoon dress she had. If she was going to sneak into someone's library, it was vital she not smudge her dress. Her absence alone might generate questions. She didn't need to see if any of her parents' footmen had Bow Runner aspirations.

Lucy grabbed her reticule, poured the gold into a silk satchel, then tucked it into her bodice. The coins were cold and hard. Lucy rushed down the servants' stairs and entered the kitchen. Maids stared at her, and she gave a tight smile. "Just—er—looking for Rose. Is she here?"

One of the kitchen maids shook her head.

"Very well then," Lucy said brightly. She'd been fully cognizant of the fact Rose wasn't here. Rose had her half day. "In that case, I'll—er—just get some air."

Lucy ducked through the kitchen door that led to the courtyard. Hopefully, the servants would merely deem her eccentric. Surely, it wouldn't occur to them that she was attempting to break into a neighboring townhouse.

She entered the garden and surveyed the courtyard. The buildings looked distinctly different from this perspective. No Grecian goddesses graced any of the doors. The townhouses were devoid of the columns and flourishes that made the other side of Grosvenor Square so unique. Even the grass was inconsistently maintained, too large in some areas and entirely devoid of grass in others.

Lucy inhaled, but no amount of air, not even the nicely scented version prevalent in this section of Mayfair with its abundance of enticingly scented flowers and bushes, could possibly lessen her nerves.

Lucy looked surreptitiously in every direction, but the courtyard was empty.

Horses-hooves clopped rhythmically on the other side of the houses, the speed perpetually languid, as if it were impossible for people in this location ever to be late to something, ever to require a doctor with urgency, or ever need to flee.

She gazed at the neighboring townhouse. That was where the Duchess of Sturbridge lived. More importantly, this was where the Duke of Sturbridge kept his library.

If there was a time for this to work, it was now, in the afternoon, after the duke would have finished his morning exercises in Hyde Park but before he began his night of debauchery. Lucy wasn't certain what rakes did at night, but suspected it kept them from their mother's homes.

Lucy rested her hand against her bodice, ensuring the coins remained secure, then hastened toward the house. If anyone looked outside, they could see her. Speed was of the essence. She didn't want to contemplate what might happen if she got caught. Would people believe she was simply one of those eccentric Americans whom people clucked their tongues at disapprovingly?

If only the Duke of Sturbridge weren't her only hope. If only she could simply read her book.

After a few short paces that seemed to last forever, she arrived. She crept by the windows. Would he be alone? She should have brought a telescope. She peered into the room, and her heart tensed.

There, on the other side of the desk, was the duke.

Heavens, the man was handsome. Somehow, she'd forgotten. Every time she saw him, she seemed struck again by the man's imposing presence. It was utterly unfair the world had managed to put so much perfection in a single man. His nose was straight, his shoulders broad, and his hair tousled and endearing.

She hesitated. Would he laugh at her proposal? She could still change her mind. There was time to dash back to the kitchen.

Still, this was her chance. He was here and he was alone.

She hurried to the window, then pushed against it.

It was locked.

Drat.

Still, it was not the only window in the room.

The next window was open. Joy surged through her. Thank goodness for bright sunny days and the need to open windows. She raised it further. *Perfect.*

The duke remained engrossed in his work.

If someone else had been in the room, she would have heard noises by now. That, at least, was good.

She glanced around. The window ledge was high. She needed a ladder or chair. Unfortunately, though there were many chairs inside the library, none were outside.

Still, she could do this. She *must* do this. She pulled herself up slowly, slowly, slowly. Her arms ached. Her stomach ached. Her back ached. She refused to let go.

Lucy fell and collided with the ground. Dirt and leaves clung to her dress. She heaved herself up, ignoring the sudden quickening of her breath.

This wasn't working.

Lucy scanned the building. There was a ledge next to the window. Perhaps she could approach from that side? She hurried past the library, then climbed onto a trellis. Wood creaked beneath her, and some strips snapped. *No matter.*

Once she reached the ledge, she climbed onto it and spread her hands, clutching the wall as best as she could. She inched to the side and refused to topple. Finally, she reached the window.

Heavens, she'd done it.

Joy was quickly halted by apprehension, but she ignored the manner in which her chest squeezed. Lucy poked her foot inside the library experimentally. Yes, the window was definitely open. She crouched on the ledge and gazed into the library.

The Duke of Sturbridge gawked at her from the other side of the window. His eyes widened, and his mouth formed a circle. With her luck, she would be featured in a *Matchmaking for Wallflowers* column, under the title "Awful American" or something similarly uncomfortable.

Lucy moved her finger hastily to her mouth.

"Shh," she hissed.

He rubbed his eyes as if, for a moment, he thought he had concocted her in his mind.

She smiled. She could *almost* take that as a compliment.

He inched toward the bell pull.

Fiddle-faddle.

She needed to stop him. *Now.*

Lucy tumbled into the room face first, bottom up, skirts . . . Well, she didn't want to think about her skirts. Thank goodness for drawers.

She scrambled up, conscious her face must be red. Her locks tumbled from her chignon despite Rose's skills with arranging her thick red hair. Evidently, Rose had not anticipated she would be diving into rooms headfirst.

Lucy lifted her chin and tried to convey some decorum.

"Miss Lucy Banks," the Duke of Sturbridge said finally.

"Yes, Your Grace." She flicked some leaves and twigs from her dress.

He narrowed his eyes. "I hope you didn't destroy the trellis outside."

"I shall pay for that," she assured him.

"What are you doing here?" His hand crept toward the bell pull.

"I wouldn't pull that if I were you."

"No?"

"No. If someone comes in, I'll tell them you were compromising me."

His eyes widened even further. "You wouldn't."

"I would."

His face whitened. The man didn't need to look so horrified at the prospect.

Lucy inhaled. "I have something to tell you, and you are going to listen."

"What do you have to tell me?" his voice creaked.

"I have a plan."

"Indeed?"

"A plan that will benefit both of us. An excellent plan."

"And what does that plan entail?"

"It entails you courting me."

He blinked.

"A false courtship."

"Only a false one?"

"Of course," she said hastily. "I wouldn't expect you to actually court me."

"Marriage with you is something I absolutely do not desire," he said.

Somehow the words hurt more than they should have, but she squared her shoulders, as if he'd said nothing more inflammatory than expressing a distaste for stewed fruit. He was being practical. She had to respect that.

"And I doubt I even like you," she replied.

That much was indeed true, no matter how handsome he was.

"I must enter a faux courtship," Lucy continued. "My sister requires me to appear to have an eminent betrothal."

"You broke into my library so your sister will be allowed to have a suitor?" His tone was wondrous.

She nodded. "Indeed. Once they become betrothed, we can halt our understanding."

He scrutinized her.

"My parents won't want the scandal of a broken engagement with her," she explained.

"People might suspect you're not untouched," the duke said finally.

"Nonsense. We'll always be chaperoned."

"I'm a very virile man. They might suspect I found a way."

"Oh." Her shoulders slumped, then she arched her chin. "Then there will be gossip. So be it. This is still the right thing to do."

"And I am your ideal candidate?"

"Yes."

"I am most people's ideal candidate," he said grumpily, but he did not tug the bell pull. That was good. There was hope. "You want me to propose to you?"

"Of course not."

Sturbridge's forehead did not move. "Every woman wants me to propose."

On another day, Lucy might have rolled her eyes. This was not that sort of day. This mattered too much.

"You're handsome," Lucy said.

Sturbridge shot her a smug look.

Lucy narrowed the distance between them. "But you also do not possess funds."

Sturbridge blinked, and his sun-kissed skin suddenly appeared pale.

"Poor enough to consider marrying someone," Lucy continued.

"And how do you know—?" The duke halted abruptly, and Lucy sighed. Clearly, the man could not even utter the word poor. The man's masculinity was evidently in full force.

"Denial is not helpful," she said in a soothing manner.

"But how—"

"Oh." She shrugged. "You live in a gentlemen's club. Clearly, you can't afford to purchase another home for you or your mother. That counts as money-deprived for dukes."

"Nonsense."

The last word seemed emphasized with unnecessary flourish. Lucy's heartbeat tightened, and she wished she had not insisted on standing.

"I'll ensure you'll never have to marry anyone."

"That's impossible," Sturbridge muttered.

"No." Lucy removed the bag of gold from her bodice and flung it on the desk. "It's not impossible."

CHAPTER SIX

Sturbridge's throat dried. Women didn't sneak into his library, display their drawers, however inadvertently, and pull gold from their bodices. Miss Banks seemed to have no idea of how distracting she was being. She leaned down, and Sturbridge averted his gaze, lest it linger on her rounded bosom.

Though Sturbridge generally had no opinion on colors, her umber dress made her face look more drained and her freckles more visible. A carriage might as well have sent a muddy puddle flying toward her face. And yet, despite all that, it was difficult not to contemplate her curves and the appealing floral scent that wafted from her.

Her dress was too tight, and he suspected she'd chosen it more for it being conducive to sneaking through courtyards than for any attempt at fashion. The curve of her bosom was impossible to ignore, and his fingers twitched, as if longing to pull her dress down even further. Would her peaks be dark pink? Or an equally appealing dusky rose color? Would they pebble beneath his touch?

Not important.

Harrison forced himself from such thoughts and eyed the gold scattered upon his desk. "You wish to pay me?"

"Indeed. There's more where that came from."

His eyebrows shot up. "There's quite a lot here."

"Yes." She smiled proudly. "There is. Still, should you require it, there's more."

Harrison gathered the coins and stacked them, enjoying the different emotions playing on Miss Banks's face. The gold coins clinked pleasurably against one another, and he built a tall tower that reached higher than the books perched on his table. Harrison knocked the middle coin down with his finger, and the coins collapsed.

Miss Lucy Banks leaned forward, and her emerald eyes sparkled. "It made quite a cheerful sound, didn't it? Money does that."

"Yes. The sound is satisfying."

"You can keep the money if you pretend to court me." Miss Banks scrunched her lips together. "I mean, obviously, you needn't call it that. I wouldn't even expect you to call at my house."

"How considerate of you. Still, you seem to be under the impression I require funds," Harrison said.

"You needn't worry. This will be our secret."

Harrison continued to study her.

He took the money and slipped it back into the pouch. The coins clanged against one another as they fell. Then he took her hand, feeling a strange heat swirling from it, despite the lace gloves she was wearing. He pressed the satchel into her hand.

A disappointed look came over her face. "I thought . . . Perhaps it was a foolish idea."

"You are under the impression I am in need of money."

Her eyes darted to the side, then she gazed at him. A look of horror fell over her face, and her wide mouth fell open. She shut it hastily. "Are you telling me, Your Grace, that you do not require funds?"

"I am a duke, after all."

"But you are a duke who lives at the Robertson's Gentlemen's Club."

"Indeed."

"It's hardly a ducal setting," Miss Banks continued. "Just various rooms."

"The Duke of Framingham lived there."

"But before he inherited the dukedom. He had hardly any money."

"I am well aware of Framingham's former financial status. It is indeed much improved of late."

"Yes, he has that whole castle in Staffordshire. I didn't think you had a castle in Staffordshire."

"No, not in Staffordshire," Harrison said, "though there is one in Cornwall. I have another castle in Surrey."

"Oh." Her faced whitened.

Her blatant shock was almost amusing. Finally, she straightened and jutted her chin out as if she were attempting to resemble the most patriotic portraits of Bonaparte. "Castles always require money. Surely you would benefit from some money."

"I don't want your pin money. Though that is a sizeable amount. Your father must be wealthy indeed."

"Yes," she said, "I will inherit much of it."

"It must be nice to not have inheritances tied to an estate and title," Harrison mused. "No sons, then?"

She shook her head, and the luxurious curls that feathered her face glinted like the flames found dancing in his fireplace. "No, no sons. Mama always said I was terrible enough."

"Your sister Isabella?"

"She's angelic, but by the time she'd grown old enough for them to be certain of that, it was too late for Mama to have more."

Harrison studied her. For a wild moment, he considered going along with her preposterous plan. Naturally, he did not require any capital, but it might be entertaining all the same to pose as her besotted beloved. Dancing with her at her balls, chitchatting with her at dinner parties, might be enjoyable. Then he could rest his hand upon her narrow waist as they waltzed, and he could inhale that delicious jasmine fragrance that clung to her skin. He would be closer to her plump, red lips, and when she laughed, and he would be certain to make her laugh, he could hear that throaty sound from her long and slender neck.

Still, it was impossible.

He strode toward her, and hope darted over her face. He steeled himself. He was going to disappoint her. But first...

"You should go," Harrison said.

Miss Banks's shoulders slumped, and Harrison resisted the sudden urge to tell her that he'd changed his mind. Her alto voice was soft. "You won't consider it?"

Harrison shook his head and refused to ponder the fact they were close enough to kiss. Since when had he thought about kissing Lucy Banks? But her succulent lips were only inches away, and he had an odd urge to delve between them. His cock was also contemplating that possibility. It strained against his tweed breeches, optimistic for release. It thrummed and pulsed and jutted up.

Egat.

"I'm sorry," he said gruffly. "You should find someone else. Or not. I wouldn't like to see you get hurt. Finding a faux suitor is not a good idea."

"But my sister—"

"It is admirable to consider her," Harrison said, "but you could be ruined if your scheme were exposed."

"I won't be exposed."

"But you could be harmed." He narrowed the distance between them still further. He could count every long dark eyelash and every delicious freckle that dotted her satin skin.

"I could?" Her alto voice faltered, and her eyes darted from his eyes to his lips, then settled to the side of the room.

He smirked and nodded solemnly. "For instance, a man might put his arms around you."

"Oh." Her verdant eyes widened, and her thick lashes swooped upward.

He rested his hands on her slender waist. The fabric of her dress was coarse, no doubt chosen more for its advantages for clambering through library windows than elegance. It lacked the allure of some ball gowns, but his fingers still sparked, as if touching the finest silk, spun from expensive caterpillars on the other side of the world.

"What might a man do then?" Her voice wobbled, and he smirked. He knew exactly what a man might do then.

He leaned nearer her and tightened his grip on her waist. Her soft bosom pressed against his chest, and the urge to pull down that dreadful dress overcame him. Would her breasts bounce were he to delve inside of her with his cock? But of course they would bounce. He itched to feel her rounded mounds with his hands. He yearned to see the exact shape of her bosom, to see the exact color of her forbidden peaks. His aching manhood jutted upward, evidently confused to be in the presence of so much magnetism and not be called to enter and thrust and explode.

"A man would kiss you," he whispered.

Lucy's luscious red lips parted, and a small breathless sigh escaped. Her lashes flickered downward.

Harrison released her from his grasp and turned away abruptly. "It will behoove to be careful."

Lucy blinked, and her cheeks flushed. Harrison resisted the urge to sweep her into his arms again, to feel every curve against his body, and to actually breech her tantalizing mouth.

She looked like she might want to say more, but finally she turned to the window and scrambled through it.

He stared after her.

The woman was unbelievable. Utterly unbelievable.

His cock still throbbed, and he glared at it. Now was not the time for it to attempt momentous endurance records.

Harrison paced the library, imagining Miss Banks would return. Even though she was no longer in the same room, the same house as him, her presence remained distracting.

Her audaciousness was almost appealing. He smiled, thinking about how she'd tumbled into the room.

Still, he could not volunteer to be her suitor. The idea was ridiculous.

Whom would she pick instead of him? There weren't many dukes about. There was, of course, the Duke of Dorchester, but he lived in Cornwall and was reclusive despite the fact he had not yet reached the age of thirty.

Harrison glanced at his desk. It was impossible to sit and gaze at his ledgers, even though he'd normally always considered that a pleasurable task. Even his estate manager had been impressed with the utter care he'd taken managing his estate's money, saying he'd never seen any aristocrat keep an estate so well-managed. Clearly, his estate manager was under the impression that the greater the title, the less care one took in money management.

Harrison exited the building. At some point, it had decided to rain, and large wet drops pattered on the pavement. Normally, he would have returned for his umbrella, but he continued on, smiling as the rain fell upon him.

Finally, he arrived at Benedict's house. He rapped on the door, and the butler showed him to Benedict's library.

Benedict gazed up at him, startled.

Harrison shifted his legs awkwardly. He was not prone to visiting Benedict in the afternoon. "I—er—came to call on you."

"How nice." Concern filled Benedict's eyes, as if he expected Harrison to announce the doctor had just told him his mother was dying.

"What are you doing now?"

"Oh." Benedict put aside his quill. "I'm writing letters.

"Very good. Good to keep correspondences going and know what's happening around the country."

Benedict's cheeks turned an unusual pink color, as if he'd just smeared rose petals over his face.

"You're not writing a letter to someone outside London," Harrison said.

Benedict shook his head. "I'm writing a letter to *her*."

"Miss Isabella Banks?"

"Yes." A blissful smile spread over his face, and his eyes took on a dewy look as he stared into the middle distance. "Isabella is the loveliest name in the world. Don't you agree?"

"It has a nice ring to it." Harrison settled into the armchair opposite Benedict's desk.

Benedict shook his head firmly. "No. Isabella sounds like angels' melodies."

"Quite," Harrison said politely. "That's a better way of putting it."

"Beethoven himself could not create music with one-tenth the sweetness of the simple sound of her name."

"Er—yes." Harrison nodded. "Well, he wouldn't attempt that anyway."

"Precisely." Benedict stood, as if Isabella's mere name were energy inducing. "Beethoven knew there would be no point even in trying. No word is lovelier than Isabella, just as no woman is fairer, sweeter than—"

"Miss Isabella Banks?" Harrison finished for him.

Benedict looked at him seriously. "I've never heard you mention a romantic interest, Harrison."

"Me?" Harrison looked around, as if Benedict could possibly have addressed a footman who'd just entered the room.

Benedict had not.

"Oh, there are many women." Harrison shifted in his seat. The leather was not as comfortable as he'd anticipated when he sat down.

"True," Benedict said. "When you dance, you always dance with many different women, but there doesn't seem to be one who's really made an impression on you."

"You find that odd?" Harrison asked.

Benedict nodded.

Harrison swallowed hard. "You exaggerate."

Indeed, it wasn't true. There had been women who'd made an impression. Women he'd admired tremendously. And there had been other women—opera singers, actresses—whom he'd also spent time with, particularly during his younger days out of university, when such goings-on were common.

Now the prospect of seducing an actress lacked the enticement it once held. When Harrison developed a tenderness for a particular woman, he'd always made a point of staying far from her. He didn't require melancholic thoughts at night. Love was clearly overrated, given the number of poets who'd experienced it and written about aches in their hearts.

"Perhaps you should meet someone," Benedict said.

"Meet someone? I meet plenty of women."

In fact, Harrison had met one of them today in his library, though he could hardly share that with Benedict.

Benedict sighed. "I would love you to have the happiness I share with Isabella."

"You're not even allowed to court her."

"And yet I'm still happy simply knowing she's alive. It's wonderful that such perfection exists. It's marvelous."

Harrison furrowed his brow. He doubted he would want to be married to perfection itself. He could always just hire some painter to make a portrait of Venus so that he might regard it all day.

Harrison bit his lip. There was a question he wanted to ask Benedict: an embarrassing question, but the answer to it might be of importance.

"Do others discuss the fact I haven't been paired with anyone? When I'm not around?"

Harrison's eyes fell on a portrait. Judging by the subject's blond cherubic curls and old-fashioned attire, he was one of Benedict's ancestors. The room heated, as if someone had swathed him in a scratchy woolen blanket.

"Oh yes. Everyone talks about your perpetually unattached status." His face sobered. "Perhaps I shouldn't have said anything. I'm sorry. I definitely shouldn't have said anything."

"No, no, it was a question," Harrison said. "I wanted to know the answer, and you told me. Thank you very much."

Benedict's shoulders relaxed, and he beamed. "I am your best friend, after all."

"Yes," Harrison said, "you are."

Benedict was right. He was Harrison's best friend, especially now Mr. Rupert Andrews had gone and married a princess. Rupert was now blissfully living at Laventhorpe Castle. He only occasionally sent letters musing about the idyllic landscape, the superior livestock that roamed there, and the utter brilliance of his wife.

If even Benedict considered it odd Harrison had not been paired with someone else, might other people be thinking that? And if they did, would one of them uncover the reason?

Harrison stiffened. That couldn't happen. He'd made a vow long ago to the duchess and wasn't going to break it now. He'd chosen a path, and he had to stay on the path, whatever happened. Perhaps, after she died, things could be different. Now, she was his only family.

"What do you think about Isabella's older sister?"

"She's hopeless." Benedict chuckled. "One wonders they're even related. Pity too, of course, since I'm not allowed to see Isabella formally until her older sister is courting someone. They know it will be difficult for the older sister to marry. I have the impression they're quite a clever family, despite all the signs to the contrary. They do speak with a deafening volume."

"Perhaps people in the United States have weaker ears."

"I hadn't considered that."

"It was a joke, Benedict," Harrison said.

"Still, something to ponder."

"There are several things to ponder."

Benedict raised his eyebrows, but Harrison quickly bowed and left the room.

Every year, the jokes magnified, and every year, Harrison grew more uncomfortable. His friends had married, and they all extolled the institution. They spoke about their children with more joy than they'd ever directed to cigars or brandy.

He couldn't let anyone suspect. Perhaps it was odd at his age to still live in a club. Could he do that ten years from now? Twenty years? Most of the people who lived in the club did so because they were in London for short periods or because they couldn't afford townhouses. Everyone knew neither situation applied to him.

Perhaps he should go abroad to halt more questions. They could assume him so passionate about travel that he had no desire to settle down. They could declare him irresponsible, even though Harrison showed responsibility in every other facet of his life. When his friends had made themselves sick when they were younger from downing alcohol at too great a speed and too great a quantity, Harrison had taken care of them.

Perhaps a faux courtship with Miss Lucy Banks would be beneficial.

Unfortunately, he'd sent her away. Harrison had made a horrible mistake.

CHAPTER SEVEN

The first step to rectifying the mistake was to find Lucy.

Fortunately, he found her at the Duchess of Hammett's ball. She wore a pale blue gown with a silver overlay. She practically shimmered.

Harrison marched toward her, ignoring the startled expressions of other guests who weren't expecting him to approach her, then swept into a deep bow. "What a pleasure to see you again."

Lucy did not smile and she gritted her teeth.

A stony expression was not his intended goal, and Harrison flinched. Still, he forced himself to continue to beam. "I thought we could have this dance."

"You amuse me, Your Grace."

"I am most amusing," he agreed, "though I wouldn't say this precise moment is a humorous one."

Lucy arched an eyebrow, and Harrison sighed. Clearly, she was upset at him for rejecting her offer. He didn't blame her.

"We are being observed," Harrison said softly. "You're supposed to take my hand, then we're supposed to dance."

"You don't have to ask me to dance. In fact, I'd rather not spend any time with you anymore at all." Lucy turned away and scrutinized a nearby painting.

If there was any artistic merit to that oil painting of one of the Duke of Hammett's relatives, Lucy would find it, given the intensity of her gaze.

Harrison shifted his legs. Previously, he might have been pleased with her willingness to avoid him.

If he'd truly asked her to dance at an effort at politeness, he might have been grateful to learn he didn't have to make forced conversation with her. Still, that was decidedly not the case now.

Too many people were asking questions, and he had no desire to make some poor young debutante think there might be a chance he would marry her and make her his Duchess of Sturbridge. Unfortunately, whenever he'd approached a woman for even a single dance, they would form odd, dewy-eyed expressions. It was kinder to stay away.

Had his mother gazed at his father with similar wonder when he had first approached her? Sturbridge's heart tightened.

When he approached women, they would stop talking entirely, smile too brightly, and giggle at everything he said.

A faux courtship was not a terrible idea. Besides, he knew Lucy's situation. He knew the bravery it had taken for her to approach him. He also knew, frankly, that she despised him.

That fact had always been clear, given the sour looks she gave her mother when her mother declared herself pleased by his presence.

He'd always thought it unfortunate that Miss Lucy Banks and her family had moved in next door to his townhouse where his mother resided in Grosvenor Square. In fact, it had been anything else but that. It had been a great boon.

"Let's dance," he said through gritted teeth.

"What?"

"I insist we dance." With that, Harrison dragged her to the dance floor. A rush of heat moved through him as he grasped her gloved hand.

Lucy's eyes widened, and her mouth formed an o. She slipped on the polished marble floor, and he righted her, noting the delightful manner in which her back curved.

"What are you doing?" She sent him a shocked look.

"Smile."

She did, and, heavens, there was something brilliant about her smile.

"You have a lovely smile."

"Is that what you came to tell me?"

"No," he said. "I have something else to discuss with you."

She raised an eyebrow.

"Your idea—"

"I hope you're not here to tell me not to find another faux suitor. I am determined."

"No," Harrison said. "As long as you're resolute on going through with it, I'm not here to sway you from your plan. Quite the contrary."

She sent him a shocked look. "You mean . . . "

He nodded. "Miss Lucy Banks, I am officially faux courting you."

"Oh." Her mouth dropped open.

"We're on the dance floor, my dear. Remember to gaze at me in a besotted manner. We find each other terribly intriguing. Everyone will think we're a thrilling couple. People will discuss us."

"Because of my poor reputation," she said in a soft voice.

"That's not what I meant. Besides, your best friend is a princess. That can't make you too unpopular."

"Some people remember that she broke into a men's club."

"That makes you scandalous by association," Harrison said. "And I, as a rake, find that appealing."

Lucy giggled. "I suppose I'm somewhat scandalous."

"No one except me knows how much," he murmured, pulling her closer to him so no one would hear.

Her cheeks pinkened. "I don't always break the rules. I am a very good girl."

He chuckled. "I will refrain from handing you tobacco."

"It is a distasteful habit."

"See," he said, "that's something we agree upon. It is a marvelous foundation for our fake courtship."

"Is that what you're going to be telling everyone when you explain we are entwined with our hearts?"

"I was hoping there might be other common points of interest I could find instead, though it is nice there's something to fall back on."

She laughed, and his heart warmed.

The dance began, and he stepped back, going into the correct pose, holding his hands just so and his legs just so. She did the same.

"I think it's quite unfair," he said, "that men's legs are constantly on display, and women get to hide their legs inside large dresses."

She giggled. "Well, there have to be some advantages to being a woman, though I've never thought this particular one was an advantage."

"No?" He questioned her.

"You see," Lucy said, "I'm an excellent dancer. I wouldn't mind if anyone saw my legs. They're quite shapely."

"Excuse me?"

Lucy bounced up and down in perfect rhythm to the Scottish reel. She was not out of breath, but her eyes sparkled and shimmered.

For a sudden moment, he imagined her legs bare, and his heartbeat quickened. "You said shapely."

"I've had many dance lessons."

"Oh," he said, "that's what you meant. Not shapely in the other sense."

"Well, they're shapely because I do so many lessons," she said.

"Oh. You meant in a purely factual manner."

"Indeed. In a purely factual manner, I have quite shapely legs."

"And I'll never see them because they're hidden in that great big skirt of yours."

She giggled. "Precisely."

Harrison smiled. "I'll have to pay attention to my dance steps to keep up with you."

"I assure you," she said, "that you are a natural."

She wasn't the first woman to compliment his dancing, but he found himself grinning.

"So, you like dancing?" He tilted his head and gazed at her. Somehow, he hadn't expected that.

"I like all activities. I like running. I like anything that involves balls."

Her plump, red lips grinned up at him, and something in his core tightened. He wasn't going to think about that. She was an innocent after all, and he was not, absolutely not, going to make a double entendre joke.

"What precisely does our fake courtship involve?" he asked.

"People should see us together at various events."

Harrison nodded. That sounded like an excellent idea, particularly when the events in question included dancing.

"We'll have to compare calendars," he said. "I hope you are planning to attend the same events as me."

"And if I'm not?" She bit her lip, perhaps thinking about how she attended less important balls, like that of Sir Seymour, and her family had not procured entry to the most exclusive establishments.

"I can visit the hosts in question and comment about how nice it would be to see you there."

She stared at him. "You would do that for me?"

"I assure you, I have much sway."

"I don't doubt that. You're the most eligible man in all London."

"Unfortunately, that's becoming all too clear to me."

"You could marry anyone," she said. "You know why I want a fake courtship, but why on earth would you, if not for the money?"

"I think we should set some rules," Harrison said, avoiding her question. "The first rule is that you cannot ask me that question."

She nodded.

"But the second rule is that we'll compare calendars and attend the same events."

"I quite prefer the second rule," she said.

"I thought you might." He smirked.

The dance continued. When it was necessary to switch partners, they parted.

A sudden longing shot through Harrison's chest as if he already missed her, even though they could only have been dancing for three minutes.

It would be easy to feign being utterly enraptured by her. He smiled. This was going to be a most marvelous season.

WHEN LUCY RETURNED to the dance, she half expected the duke to smile and say he'd simply been jesting. He did smile, but he didn't say he was jesting.

Her skin warmed at his touch, as if he'd swept her away to some glorious Mediterranean country filled with sunbeams and not simply onto a dance floor filled with people she didn't particularly like.

The other dancers' eyes bored into her, and she shivered. Eyebrows lurched, and mouths dropped.

"Everyone's watching us," Lucy said.

"Naturally." The duke's eyes shimmered.

"You're well aware of your own importance."

"Mmhmm," the duke agreed nonchalantly, evidently not seeing it as important to speak actual words.

But then, the duke hardly needed to speak. He was already perfect. His glossy hair glowed in the flickering candlelight. Caramel strands mixed with darker ones, and she had an odd urge to trace them with her fingers. His high cheekbones made his face appear more chiseled, more thoughtfully composed than the others in the room. He was taller than most of the guests as well, and Lucy felt small and insignificant beside him. He would probably look immaculate if he danced with a vase of flowers or one of the brooms the maids used.

Some older women stared at them, puzzlement evident on their faces. Perhaps they'd tried to matchmake him with their exquisitely trained and red-hair devoid daughters.

"Now, we must get to work on our contract," the duke said. "This is my first time doing this."

"And you're already a natural."

He gave a modest shrug. "I create contracts sometimes for my estate. In fact, I'm having a house party at Thornridge Castle to celebrate the end of the season. Perhaps I could invite you and your family there."

"Oh."

"Is something wrong?"

"I assumed this would end at the end of the season."

"It could, should you prefer."

She shook her head. "No, I would quite like to see your estate. I'm certain my sister would be pleased if you invited Lord Brooke."

Harrison grinned. "I have already invited him."

"Then it would be perfect."

"Excellent."

The music ended, Lucy curtsied, and Harrison bowed.

"I will dance with you one more time later tonight," he said. "Three times would be scandalous. I'm not certain it would be believable. Twice would just be enough to intrigue people."

"Very well."

"Save me the next reel. You danced it marvelously."

Her eyes shimmered, as if still bouncing and twirling. "Thank you."

"I would almost think you were Scottish."

"My father is Scottish. He was born in Glasgow."

"He came to New York as a young child?"

"Indeed. With both parents and three siblings."

"And his family preferred New York?"

"His family wasn't hungry in New York."

"That would be an improvement."

"And now he's rich. That's even more of an improvement."

He nodded thoughtfully. "I think I like New York."

She must have been looking at him strangely, for he arched an eyebrow. "What are you thinking? Do you have any doubts?"

"No." She shook her head. "I think you'll be ideal."

His eyes sparkled, and her cheeks heated.

"You do have a very nice bow," Lucy added hastily.

"And your curtsey is superb." He grinned and led her away from the dance floor.

They separated, and people rushed toward Lucy.

"How was the dance?" one woman asked, her eyelashes fluttering. "He's so athletic. Isn't he? It must have been quite nice to dance with him."

"He is a good dancer," Lucy said.

The fact was not surprising. Most men here were good dancers. Even the dullest aristocrat in London attended a ball once a week, and the people who truly enjoyed festivities found ways to dance more often. They had hours to practice their dance steps, which always remained the same. There were only a certain number of songs in rotation.

People danced at home as well, but the men often worked on Wall Street. They were focused on creating wealth and not on perfecting basic dance skills.

Still, she had to admit the duke was *particularly* gifted at dancing.

She smiled.

She hadn't liked lingering on the corners of dance floors. Perhaps some men hadn't been confident she would know the dance steps because she was American. Maybe others had no wish to attempt to lead some overly tall woman around the floor, particularly given her association with the princess. Harrison, though, was taller than she. His height was perfect. He was perfect.

CHAPTER EIGHT

"The Duke of Sturbridge is here." The butler's voice boomed through the townhouse, and Mama straightened immediately. A wide smile dashed across her face.

"Heavens. He must be here to see Mr. Banks. Do send Mr. Banks in immediately." Mama fluffed her hair. "How very kind of the duke to drop by."

"Yes." Lucy's heartbeat pattered. The duke was here. She hadn't dreamed last night: he had agreed to her plan.

"I know his mother's house is next door, but it is such a kind gesture to check on us."

"Indeed." Lucy attempted to smile, but nervousness thrummed through her. She smoothed her dress hastily.

"Oh dear, we've quite forgotten to set out any sweets," Mama said mournfully. "What will the duke think of us? The English already think we're cannibals."

"I'm certain that's not a common belief."

"We could be cannibals for all the duke knows. He hasn't been to New York. He would have mentioned if he'd been."

Footsteps clinked across the marble floor. Footsteps that made her heartbeat quicken.

"The sweets!" Mama dashed to the bell pull and yanked it firmly. The bell pull dropped into her hands, and she stared at the fabric. "That was not supposed to happen."

"His Grace, the Duke of Sturbridge," the butler announced.

Mama's face paled, and she tightened her grip around the broken bell pull.

"Ladies." The duke swept into a deep, elegant bow. He tilted his head. "You're sewing something quite interesting, Mrs. Banks. Is it a belt?"

"Me, sew a belt out of this fabric?" Mama shook her head hastily, and her carefully coiled locks appeared rather less carefully coiled. "Though that is quite an idea."

"I'm certain it would make a nice belt," Sturbridge said.

Heavens, the man was gallant.

Mama gave the duke a shocked smile, then giggled. "No, this is our bell pull. It toppled off. Dreadfully embarrassing."

"Let me assist you." The duke marched to Mama and examined the bell pull. "We can reattach this." He gazed at the ceiling, where part of the bell pull still dangled. "Though perhaps a chair is necessary."

Sturbridge headed to a small table where Lucy sometimes wrote letters and picked up a chair.

"No chairs," Mama said hastily. "I heard what happened to the Duke of Sandridge. He was on a chair fixing something, and it broke."

Sturbridge put the chair down. "Oh, yes."

"I would not want you to fall on your bottom," Mama continued. "It's probably a very nice bottom already. Not that we should be discussing a duke's bottom, of course. I hope you don't think we go about discussing bottoms in general."

"Mama!" Lucy exclaimed.

Papa strode into the room. "What's all this?"

"We're discussing whether the duke should stand on the chair," Mama said. "I wouldn't want him to collapse onto the floor."

Papa blinked, then nodded, evidently finding no flaw in Mama's desires. "Ah. Quite sensible of you." He hesitated. "Is there a reason why we think he would fall?"

"No, absolutely no reason at all. My friend Sebastian might be clumsy with chairs, but I do not share his difficulties." Sturbridge grabbed the chair, marched toward the bell pull, and set the chair underneath it. He took the broken bell pull from Mama and held it up. "I could tie it, but some sewing would make it last longer." He looked around. "Miss Lucy Banks, do you have a needle and thread?"

"Oh, she's always sewing something. Hats, scarves, she's quite a talented daughter," Mama chattered. "My daughter Isabella is also quite talented. All my daughters are talented."

Lucy rushed over with her sewing utensils.

"Thank you." Sturbridge took her sewing box from her and fiddled with it.

Lucy's eyes widened. Surely the duke did not mean to sew the broken bell pull himself?

Sturbridge expertly threaded the needle without the eye scrunching and brow furrowing Lucy would have anticipated, and in the next moment, he was sewing the broken bell pull back together.

"My!" Mama put her hand to her heart and craned her neck upward. "You're quite good."

"Mm-hmm." The duke moved slowly but methodically, and a smile played on his lips, as if he found the task enjoyable.

He seemed unstrained by the awkward position his hands were in.

In fact, Lucy was grateful he fixed the bell pull. It would have been a struggle for anyone else.

"This isn't the first time you've sewn," Mama said.

The duke's face sobered, and Lucy wondered what he was thinking. Then he smiled again. "We dukes have multiple talents."

"Yes," Mama said. "That's becoming quite clear. Most admirable. Most, most admirable, though quite distressing that it broke. I'm utterly mortified."

The duke jumped elegantly from the chair and carried it back to the table. "It was a pleasure."

Papa stood before the bell pull, then yanked it tentatively. The bell pull did not topple into his hand, and he craned his neck, examining the duke's stitches. Finally, he grinned. "You did an excellent job."

"That was my intention," the duke said.

The housekeeper rushed into the room, evidently having heard the bell pull.

"Oh Mrs. Dowdling, I am sorry," Mama said, "but we must have sweets. The Duke of Sturbridge is here."

"Do you care for tea as well?" Mrs. Dowdling asked.

Mama nodded her head violently. "Yes, tea would be wonderful." She turned to the duke. "Unless you are a chocolate or coffee drinker? We have multiple options."

"Tea would be wonderful," the duke said, and Mrs. Dowdling scampered from the room.

Mama gestured to an armchair. "Do take a seat, Your Grace."

Papa sat on the sofa beside Mama. He plopped his shoes on the peach-tufted ottoman and put his arms casually behind his head. "It is nice to see you again."

Mama scowled at Papa's feet, then rose. "This is a gentlemen's conversation."

"Actually, I came to see Lucy." The duke fixed his gaze on Lucy.

Even though Lucy knew this was a faux courtship, even though she was absolutely certain of the fact, her heart leaped. No doubt, the duke could add acting to his many varied skills.

"You came to see *Lucy?*" Mama's voice had never sounded so startled.

The duke winked at Lucy. "Indeed."

"Heavens." Mama turned to Papa. "This is the first time Lucy has had a gentleman caller. We must be certain to celebrate."

"Mrs. Dowdling's already bringing sweets up," Papa reminded her.

"Sweets?" Mama shook her head in disgust. "Cook must make a cake."

Lucy's face reddened. Had Mama just told the duke she'd never ever had a gentlemen caller in her life?

The duke grinned, evidently finding the entire situation amusing.

Lucy's skin heated as if Mama had thrown her into the fireplace, and she sank into the sofa. If it had any power to swallow her up, now was definitely the time for it to show its magical prowess.

"Your Grace." Mama clapped her hands. "Do tell me. What is your favorite flavor of cake? Cook is an expert at all of them."

The duke rubbed his chin as if Mama had just asked him the best way to secure peace. "Something that can be made quickly."

"Ah, yes. Quickly. Good thought. Lucy, this man is brilliant."

"I am." The duke gave a broad grin.

Lucy debated tossing a pillow at him. Smacking him would be appropriate.

Mama hurried away, evidently eager to confer with Cook.

Papa scrutinized the duke. "Why are you calling on Lucy? Don't tell me this is a romantic thing. Should I get out my shotgun?"

"That won't be necessary." Sturbridge's expression lacked its earlier confidence.

"You should know I do have shotguns here," Papa said.

"Noted."

"I'm quite good at using them too."

"I see."

"Some people might not think that," Papa explained. "After all, I live in New York City and am a banker."

"Very appropriate for your name."

"I found it inspirational myself." Papa leaned back, and a pleased expression darted over his face, unencumbered by his wrinkles and sideburns. "But I can use a shotgun as good as any hungry farmer who sees a deer rushing through his fields."

"It's illegal to shoot deer here. They belong to the royals."

"Then I would do it furtively."

"I see."

"I'm certain I could sneak up without anyone noticing."

"That seems to be a family trait," the duke remarked drily.

"Excuse me?" Papa asked.

The duke shook his head. "Nothing. Not important."

"Well, I could slaughter the duke—I meant, the deer while the deer slept. Do you get my point?"

"Yes, I do."

"Papa," Lucy pleaded, "you mustn't speak of such things. He'll think you're serious."

"I am serious," Papa said. "I'm a very serious man. Everyone says so."

It was true. Everyone did say that Papa was serious, but he acted quite silly at home.

Mama soon arrived. "We're going to have a strawberry tart."

"Ah, excellent choice," the duke said.

She settled on the couch. "Now, what have you been talking about when I've been gone?"

"I have been discussing your husband's gift with weapons," the duke said.

"Oh." Mama giggled. "Well, it's a good thing I left that conversation. That sounds most dull."

"It wasn't."

Mama laughed. "You are so polite."

"Now, tell me," the duke said. "I was wondering what Lucy's schedule was for this coming few months."

Mama's eyes goggled. "You were?"

"I wanted to make sure that you were attending all the best balls."

"How very considerate." Joy sprang over Mama's face, and the duke's lips curled.

Something made her heart ache, and for the first time, Lucy wasn't certain she was doing the right thing.

CHAPTER NINE

The streets had long since calmed, the strong sunlight had shifted to its evening display of pink and lilac, and Lucy scrutinized herself in the mirror. It was something she was not unique in doing: Rose, Mama and Isabella were also staring at her.

"You needn't watch me dress," Lucy said.

"I must!" Mama insisted. "You might be tempted to sit down and rumple all Rose's efforts. Perhaps you might even lie down and destroy your chignon."

"I wouldn't do that."

Still, the idea was not dreadful. Her bed was generally a comfortable place to be. She stared at her reflection. "Do you think my hair has too many curls?"

"Nonsense. It's impossible to have too many curls in one's hair."

Lucy scrunched her lips together. She was less confident in the veracity of that statement, despite Mama's insistence.

"Everyone will be looking at me when I enter," Lucy said miserably.

"Good," Mama said. "Then the duke will be certain to find you."

Lucy's hair always resembled a beacon, and she scowled. "I'm certain he'll find me anyway."

Mama beamed. "My sweetheart. I am so happy to see you so confident."

"Perhaps the duke is already falling in love," Isabella declared.

"Truly?" Mama clapped her hands together.

"I—I." Lucy swallowed hard. This was the plan she'd concocted, but guilt moved through her. "We'll see."

The statement was tepid, but Mama's eyes still sparkled, as if Lucy had just declared that she'd seen Cupid himself and had been struck by his arrow.

"It's simply a poetry reading," Lucy said.

"A poetry reading that he insisted you attend as well," Mama said. "I can't imagine anything more romantic than poetry. It's an excellent sign that he wanted to make certain that you attend it."

"I think so too," Isabella said. "In fact... Do you think I might be able to have a suitor too?"

Mama frowned. "The duke invited Lucy to a poetry reading. That's not a marriage proposal. We must see how the night proceeds."

Isabella's smile faltered, and she drew back.

"He invited me to other things as well," Lucy said hastily.

"Yes, he did." Mama's face brightened, and she chattered about the superiority of poetry over all other forms of writings and its marvelous ability to cause hearts to lurch and patter with ferocity.

Indeed, Lucy's heart was lurching now, though it was only from nervousness. Finally, even Mama declared Lucy ready, and they proceeded toward Haviland Place.

Isabella and Lucy strode beside each other, following Mama and Papa. Her parents' noisiness and ability to make vast amounts of money were equaled only by their energy and their tendency to stride swiftly.

"I can't believe I missed the duke's presence," Isabella said. "And to think he called on you. Darling Benedict must have lauded your virtues."

"Perhaps." Lucy decided not to tell Isabella she'd offered to pay the duke to pretend to court her. That was the sort of thing one kept private.

Lucy moved stiffly, conscious of the tightness of her stays. They dug into her shift with an unpleasant force.

The duke had confirmed he would be at Haviland Place, and Mama had insisted on Lucy looking immaculate. Unfortunately, looking immaculate did not preclude being uncomfortable, and that was the case now.

Finally, they reached Haviland Place. Lucy stepped into the townhouse. Ornate blue-and-white chinoiserie vases were perched on dainty sideboards with gilded legs. Heavy silver mirrors rested on sideboards, as if to make certain each expression of good taste was seen.

Isabella pointed to a set of shining armor clutching an ax. "That looks threatening."

"Quite convenient for burglars if they forgot their weapons at home."

Isabella giggled. "You mustn't say such things. I'm not supposed to laugh here. This is a very serious place."

"Indeed?"

"It's a poetry reading. What could be more serious than that?" Isabella's eyes shone. She adored poetry readings.

Personally, Lucy thought they were rubbish. She would far rather attend a lecture on some scientific happening than hear words strewn together describing platitudes, typically extolling the aesthetic value of flowers.

"It won't be terrible," Isabella assured her.

"It won't be good," Lucy said, suddenly nervous about meeting Sturbridge. How would she keep her heart from pitter-pattering at his presence? He'd been so pleasant toward her parents yesterday, talking at length with them.

"The Duke of Sturbridge is waving," Isabella said.

"Splendid." Lucy's voice squeaked, but she waved back.

A few people turned in their direction.

"You must have made quite an impression on him during those dances," Isabella said. "Our dance instructor would be very proud."

"Perhaps it was not my feet the duke was admiring."

Isabella's eyes rounded, and Lucy giggled.

"I'm going to greet him." Lucy moved past women wearing dresses with enormous puffed sleeves. The hems were adorned with ribbons and flounces. This might not be a ball, but no one could doubt the importance of this social occasion.

Finally, Lucy reached the duke. He'd procured a place at the front of the room and gestured to a seat.

"We meet again." The duke's voice rumbled in her ear.

Lucy sat beside him, conscious of people's stares. She focused on sitting straight, as if it was perfectly normal to sit beside a duke.

But he wasn't just a duke. He was a handsome duke.

Murmurings around her grew, humming like a hive of bees.

This was just what she had wanted. They were being noticed. Her plan was working perfectly. Soon Mama would have to let Isabella become betrothed with her viscount.

"Your eyes are shining," he said.

"Perhaps."

He chuckled. "I'm not sure they'll be shining much after this performance."

"You don't expect it will be very good?"

"Not if you have poetic inclinations," he said.

He was right.

The poetry was histrionic, despite the enthusiasm with which the countess spoke about the poet's skills, but Harrison's presence beside her occupied her mind more than even the most adeptly arranged sonnets could achieve.

THE POETRY READING at Haviland Place turned into more poetry readings. Harrison had danced with Lucy at Vauxhall, strolled with her through Hyde Park, and asked sufficient hostesses to include her and her family at dinner parties to give everyone the impression they were courting.

Harrison's favorite events remained balls. There was something delightful about dancing with Lucy in his arms. But then, even poetry readings and lectures were amusing with Lucy beside him.

Fortunately, tonight was a ball. Harrison strode through the heavy wooden doors that led to the ballroom, flanked by wig-wearing footmen, and joined the throng of partygoers.

He surveyed the guests, looking for Lucy's vibrant hair.

Tonight, he saw Mrs. Banks first. Her cobalt turban, complete with peacocks and jewels, helped.

Mrs. Banks rushed toward him, dragging her husband and daughters. Her puffed sleeves wobbled at the sudden force. No doubt, the dressmaker had not anticipated the vigor of Mrs. Banks's strides.

"Your Grace!" Mrs. Banks exclaimed. "How delightful to see you!"

Harrison opened his mouth to convey his similar pleasure at seeing her, but Mrs. Banks continued to chatter and pointed. "Is that your mother? The duchess? We must meet her."

Harrison's heart sank.

Mrs. Banks turned to her husband. "Don't you agree, Mr. Banks?"

Mr. Banks nodded languidly, but he gave a longing look at the book he'd evidently smuggled inside. Harrison almost admired the man's optimism. He seemed to perpetually believe he would be able to accomplish work. Hostesses usually made that possibility very unlikely.

Mrs. Banks clapped her hands. "Oh, you must take us to her and introduce us. It will be so nice to meet her."

"Yes," Mr. Banks agreed. "I find it's always advantageous to observe a person's parents. One can learn so many things that way."

Harrison's chest tightened, and his mouth dried.

"Oh, Papa, it's truly not necessary. Can't you see he's embarrassed?" Lucy pleaded.

"He's embarrassed about his mother? A duchess? I've never heard of anything quite so ridiculous." Mrs. Banks shook her head. "Though children, when you feel I am embarrassing you, just know if I were a duchess, you would still find me embarrassing. Isn't it so, Your Grace? I'm certain she's not that frightful."

"And if she is, well, I'm sure you can think of something embarrassing to even things out," Mr. Banks said with a smile.

"Yes." Mrs. Banks beamed. "I'm quite happy to spill my drink on myself if it would make you feel better."

Mr. Banks shot a nervous look at the glass of mahogany liquid his wife was carrying. "Surely that's unnecessary."

"To ease some embarrassment, it might be necessary."

"You're wearing white. You don't want a sherry stain on your dress," Mr. Banks said. "That dress is from Paris."

"We can always visit Paris again," Mrs. Banks said blithely.

"Perhaps it would be best," Harrison suggested, "to only spill something on your dress if my mother does the same?"

"Oh, you are wise, Your Grace." Mrs. Banks giggled. "I think that's the way to go. See Mr. Banks, we have a plan. I will only spill something on my dress if his mother spills something on her dress."

"What if she spilled something on your dress?" Mr. Banks mused.

"Well, in that case, I would—" she bit her lip. "Well, I would probably spill something on her dress to be even, but I wouldn't like to do that."

"Quite good," Mr. Banks said. "Duchess's dresses are apt to be expensive."

"Though," Mrs. Bank's continued, "it might be preferable if I were simply to spill something on my dress."

"So, you would have two stains on your dress then?"

Mrs. Banks nodded eagerly. "She couldn't feel guilty about marring my dress then. Now, Your Grace, will you lead us to meet your mother?"

"It's truly not necessary," Lucy rushed to say.

"It's fine," Harrison said.

This was part of their arrangement. It hadn't been something they'd specifically planned, but if they were truly courting, it would make sense for him to introduce her parents to his mother.

"She can be snippety," Harrison warned.

"Snippety? Are you saying disagreeable things about your mother in front of us?" Mrs. Banks narrowed her eyes. "That is not something a good son does."

Harrison gave a wry smile. "I just meant if she isn't pleasant, it wouldn't be your fault."

"I'm certain she's delightful," Mrs. Banks said. "Utterly."

"I hope so," Harrison muttered. He led them to the duchess, conscious of his heart quaking.

As he narrowed the distance between them, the duchess noticed them immediately. A look of displeasure passed over her face, and he tensed.

CHAPTER TEN

Harrison approached the tall, well-dressed blonde woman. Strands of pearl necklaces swept around her neck, the pale color contrasting against her regal indigo gown. The somber jewels always suited her. The Duchess of Sturbridge always looked immaculate, and tonight was no exception.

"Mother," Harrison said.

Her pale eyebrows swept upward, and her eyes landed on the Banks family.

A sour taste invaded Harrison's throat, but he forced himself to smile. "I would like to introduce you to Mr. and Mrs. Banks and their daughter, Miss Banks, and their other daughter, Miss Isabella Banks."

"So many people." The duchess moved her hand to her heart in an elegant, practiced motion. Her mouth dropped open, slightly forming a perfect O shape.

"It is a pleasure," Mrs. Banks exclaimed. "We've been so happy to see how much your son has taken to our daughter."

His mother's eyebrows lurched even higher, and Harrison had the distinct feeling this action was not practiced. She surveyed Lucy, running her gaze over her with the expertise of a modiste challenged to make a dress without procuring any measurements by hand.

Lucy shivered, and her face pinkened. Even her chin wobbled.

Damnation.

He shot a warning look at the duchess.

"How quaint," the duchess said icily. "You're an American."

"I am," Lucy said.

"Utterly amusing. No wonder my dear son is taken with you. He must find it astonishing to hear the manner you mispronounce simple words."

Lucy blinked.

"Don't you find the way she speaks most curious, my dear Harrison?" the duchess continued.

Harrison jutted out his chin. "I don't find it curious at all."

"Well, that must not be the reason why my son is intrigued by you then." Her eyes narrowed. "One does wonder what the reason must be. Certainly, I can't tell. There are so many."

"Mother." Harrison had a steely edge to his voice he hoped the duchess heard.

She laughed. "You must forgive me. It's quite late, and I am quite old. I tire easily."

Mrs. Banks shot a worried look at Mr. Banks.

Harrison despised this. Why must the duchess be so rude to the Banks? They hadn't done anything to her. And yet he knew exactly why: she did not want him to marry. Well, she didn't have to worry about that.

"Mr. and Mrs. Banks are visiting England with their daughters for a brief time." Harrison hoped the duchess would take notice of the word brief and decide not to waste any more time making snide comments as if she were a soldier whose only method of fighting was to use the vilest words.

"What do you make of London?" the duchess asked. "Where are you from?"

"New York," Mr. Banks said.

"New York, how very quaint. How adorable."

"There is nothing adorable about New York," Mr. Banks said stiffly.

"No? Perhaps you haven't been paying attention to it."

"My mother hasn't forgiven the former colonies for rebelling all those years ago," Harrison said hastily.

The duchess laughed and flapped her fan. "On the contrary, we scarcely gave any resources in our fight to keep them. Had we done so, naturally, they would have remained. Who could care about something so meager? There weren't any sugar plantations on the land, after all. We retained our Caribbean colonies."

"If you read the newspapers, you might find the former colonies are not that weak, after all," Mr. Banks said.

"Is that so?" The duchess gave him a hard stare. "How curious. I suppose that's what the newspapers in your country would print."

Harrison decided to ignore her statement. Instead, he turned to Lucy. "Perhaps, Miss Banks, we could have this dance?"

Lucy appeared startled, as if she'd half expected him to say he was entirely too busy to dance. But she nodded, and he led her to the dance floor, leaving her family with the duchess.

"I'm certain it's a bad idea to leave them there together." Harrison glanced toward Lucy's parents, who appeared to still be attempting stilted conversation with the duchess. "I couldn't bear to remain."

"They'll be fine. We Americans are a tough people, after all."

He snorted. "I believe that."

They waited at the side of the dance floor for people to finish their dance.

"She didn't seem pleased to meet us," Lucy said.

"You're correct," he admitted reluctantly.

"Is there someone else she wants you to be matched with?" Lucy's voice trembled for some reason, and he turned to her sharply, but she was examining the floor.

"No one in particular. In fact, she's quite pleased with how things are."

She tilted her head. "I see."

"In other words, you have no competition, my dear."

She giggled, and his heart soared.

The musicians switched to a waltz, and he led her onto the dance floor, then held her in his arms. They spun to the music. Normally, he wasn't fond of waltzing. It was more pleasurable, he'd always thought, to do a reel and leap about the dance floor in rhythm.

Now they glided along, but nothing about the waltz felt dull or boring now. The candles in the large candelabras flickered pleasantly and the whole room sparkled, aided by the hostess's insistence on gilding much of the walls as if she were trying to rival the walls of French nobility in the last century.

"You should laugh more often," he told her.

"Oh?"

For some reason, her face sobered, and he regretted saying anything. "Only if you find things amusing."

"Then you're not suggesting I become an actress."

He shook his head rapidly. "Certainly not."

"I'll resist the temptation to run off on the stage and perform—"

"Comedies," he finished. "Tragedies would have you crying more often, which, though also unpleasant, was not the particular situation I wanted you to avoid."

She grinned. "You're rambling."

"Perhaps." He spun her around. "I'm new to being a faux suitor."

"You'll be an expert the next time a woman sneaks into your library, trying to hand you some money to court her."

He chuckled. "That's true."

"You can write me a letter about it when I'm back in New York," she said softly.

He nodded. Suddenly, he didn't think it was a very good idea for her to return to New York.

The waltz ended, and they waited for a new dance. The air seemed thicker than before, and her delicious jasmine scent wafted around him.

A fast-tempoed song began, and they joined the other dancers in a cotillion. They parted, and he watched her dance with the other dancers, observing the manner in which her coiled red locks bounced. He suddenly had an urge to feel her locks against his fingers.

Finally, they reached each other again.

"You're beautiful," he said.

Her eyes sparkled, and she gazed around.

No one though was in earshot, and puzzlement drifted over her face.

He frowned slightly. She shouldn't think he'd only said that for the benefit of other people. "That shade of green suits you. It matches your eyes."

She smiled awkwardly.

Perhaps it was best to change the discussion.

"It's nice you're so close to your mother," Lucy said.

He raised his eyebrows. "Is that so?"

"Yes," she said.

"Are you close with your mother?"

Lucy shot a glance toward her mother, as if worried her mother might suddenly be imbued with superior hearing powers. "Not in particular."

"I'm actually not that close with my mother," he said.

"You're letting her live in your place on Grosvenor Square."

"I'm quite fond of the Robertson's Gentlemen Club," Harrison insisted.

"Indeed?"

"Yes. Everything is nearby, including a whole group of people with whom to converse. Nothing is ever dull."

"Is that important to you?" She gazed at him, and he averted his eyes, conscious of their bright emerald color. It would be too easy to stare into them.

He mused over her question. Dullness might lead to thoughts, and thoughts might lead to memories he'd vowed to forget. "Sometimes it's nice to converse."

She nodded. "I suppose so."

He felt an odd sense of disappointment, as if he'd missed an opportunity to share more with her, even though he avoided sharing things with anyone.

CHAPTER ELEVEN

Lucy separated from the duke and made her way toward her parents, conscious of people's stares.

"You've managed to keep your dress stain-free," a female voice said.

Lucy stiffened and turned.

Lady Letitia rolled her gaze over her, and Lucy stiffened.

Lady Letitia had already done multiple seasons, a fact that might have made her a cautionary tale, were she less elegant or beautiful. Instead, Lady Letitita's experience only served to bolster her standing. She knew everyone and seemed to perpetually smirk whenever she saw Lucy, as if detailing the things wrong with Lucy brought her inexplicable joy.

Now though, no smirk was on her face.

"The duke just danced with you."

"Yes," Lucy replied, "that's true."

"But he's a duke."

"Indeed." Lucy's lips twitched, and she struggled not to laugh.

Confusion continued to build on Leticia's face, marring its otherwise perfection.

"Even the duke desires to dance from time to time," Lucy said.

"Not very often," Leticia said, "and not . . . " Leticia bit her tongue and did not say *with you*.

The words may as well have been uttered.

Lady Letitia narrowed her eyes. "Why is the duke so eager to dance with *you?*"

"Because he enjoys it." Lucy raised her chin. That, certainly, was true.

Lady Letitia shook her head. "I doubt it. That man has made a point of never dancing more than one dance with a woman for years. And now he brings your parents to speak with his mother?"

"Men can change."

"Not for *you.*"

Suddenly, Lucy felt very cold. Lady Letitia continued to assess her, and Lucy had a horrible thought that Lady Letitia might *know*.

That was ridiculous.

She couldn't know. No one did.

Lucy gave Leticia a bright smile, as if she had not just said things that had made her heartrate quicken.

She spotted the duke at the punch table and sauntered toward him.

Harrison grinned. "I just saw you."

"I'm sorry. I—"

He laughed and handed her a drink. Bubbles bounced merrily from the crystal flute. "I expect there will be an article about us in next week's edition of *Matchmaking for Wallflowers.*"

"We've managed to shock some people," Lucy said.

"I have something of a reputation," he said, faux-modestly.

She raised her eyebrows. "I thought your reputation involved a lot of scowling."

"That's yours."

"The plan is working." He clinked her glass with his. "Congratulations, my dear."

Lucy took a hasty sip of the cocktail, enjoying the slight alcoholic taste. The burn, unfortunately, did not distract her from Sturbridge. Doubtless, few things could.

Sturbridge tilted his head. "Is something wrong?"

"Wrong?" Lucy's voice squeaked, and she shook her head. "Naturally not."

"Are you certain?" Sturbridge's velvety voice sounded at her ear.

Lucy sighed. When had Sturbridge known her so well?

"One of the other women, Lady Letitia, was doubtful why you wanted to spend so much time with me."

"That's ridiculous," Harrison said. "I hope you told her that."

"I don't think she believed me."

"Well." Harrison shrugged. "It doesn't matter what she thinks."

Lucy struggled to nod. "Indeed."

"Egad." A sour look descended upon Harrison's face, one not relieved when he took another sip of the sweet punch. "It does matter, doesn't it?"

"Her opinion *is* highly regarded."

"Not by me." Harrison snorted. "You should hear the Duke of Sandridge speak about her. I suppose I should invite her to my house party at Thornridge Castle."

"Whatever for?"

"So she can see that I'm utterly besotted with you." Harrison's eyes shimmered, and his breath wafted over her.

Her nostrils flared involuntarily, and she inhaled his citrus scent. Her eyes flickered shut, before she remembered to keep them open.

He grinned. A waltz started to play. "May I have this dance?"

HARRISON SET DOWN HIS punch, enjoying seeing Lucy's eyes widen.

"We've just had our dance," Lucy said.

"Do you mean to say you've already tired of me?" He raised an eyebrow.

"No! Naturally not. I—" Lucy's skin immediately pinkened, and he resisted the urge to trace the color on her cheeks.

He offered her his hand, and she grasped it. A surge of heat rushed through him at their touch, and soon he swept her into his arms for a waltz.

He guided her toward the windows on the other side of the ballroom, swirling her around to the music.

"What are you doing?"

"I thought we could enjoy the full feel of the dance floor."

"But that's not how one dances. At least not if one dances properly."

"I'm not always proper. And neither are you."

"I'm always proper," she insisted.

"You sneaked into a duke's townhouse."

"Technically, your mother's townhouse."

"I'm not certain that makes much of a difference in the eyes of people."

"It should. There was a female in the house."

"There was no female in the room except you. That's difficult for me to forget."

She stared at him in puzzlement. Heavens, she was such an innocent. She was nothing like the opera singers and actresses with their knowing smiles, their easy references to various parts of their bodies. Meeting them had been at first exciting and then, as he grew older, dull. No, he could leave actresses for the young aristocrats straight out of Cambridge or Oxford to enjoy. He needed no more part in them, but he needed her.

In the next moment, he stopped before a balcony window.

"Is Lady Letitia watching?" he murmured.

She tilted her head. "I-I think so."

"Excellent." He led her behind the jacquard drapes, then opened the balcony door. "Follow me."

Moonlight splashed over Lucy, and he focused his attention on his surroundings, taking in the dark shapes of the garden below, and the floral scent that wafted up. This was for pretend, after all. She wasn't actually his lover. He wasn't actually going to kiss her.

"I don't think we're supposed to be alone here," Lucy said.

"We can go inside whenever you want. I thought we could come here to make this courtship seem more realistic."

She straightened immediately and was all business. He grinned. Sometimes she resembled her father.

"You're hoping one of the gossipers will think we're here by ourselves doing unthinkable things together."

"Precisely."

Moonlight shone over her face. Her features were perfect and exquisite, as if they'd been sculpted from the finest marble by the most gifted sculptor. He longed to taste her.

He narrowed the distance between them, conscious of a slight scent of jasmine emanating from her skin. It was almost distracting, but he had something else on his mind. He peered toward the garden, but there were no sounds.

"You're standing awfully close," she said, and her voice trembled.

"That is how close people stand when they are courting."

"Oh?" her voice wobbled.

He ran his fingers along her jaw, then he ran them through a curl of her hair. He twirled the silky auburn strand in his hand.

"If I were your beloved, I would kiss you right now," he said.

"Then be my beloved," Lucy murmured.

"Do you mean that?" Harrison's voice sounded husky.

Kissing Lucy had absolutely been on his mind.

She drew back. "I'm sorry. I know you're just acting, I—"

Harrison pulled her back to him, then kissed her.

LUCY WAS BEING KISSED. Truly, truly kissed. Harrison's large arms clutched her in his arms. A woodsy scent wafted about her. The wind was calmer here, evidently hindered by the tall hedges that surrounded them. Harrison's manor house was no longer visible.

There was only Harrison.

Her heartbeat quickened.

Harrison wasn't supposed to be kissing her. Faux beloveds didn't kiss each other. Perhaps they might do so if they were discovered underneath mistletoe, and they were somehow obligated to prove their affection, but they wouldn't kiss otherwise.

They certainly wouldn't kiss in privacy. Not every engaged couple kissed in privacy.

She pulled away, conscious of his firm hands still holding her. "You don't need to do this."

He studied her, and heat surged through her. It was tempting to melt into his arms, to pretend he truly cared for her, to pretend they were truly lovers. She wanted to lean against his sturdy chest as if it were her safe haven, and she wanted to kiss his succulent lips.

They were not truly lovers though, and she stepped away.

"What's wrong?" he asked.

"You've very nice," she said, "but..."

"But?"

She raised her chin. She wasn't going to avert her gaze. "I'm fine. You needn't pity kiss me."

He widened his eyes. "You think I go about giving pity kisses?"

The air suddenly grew thicker, even though they remained outside.

"Perhaps?"

"I assure you that I do not do that," he said, his voice stern.

"Perhaps you don't give pity kisses to everyone, but..."

"You think I give them solely to you?"

She blinked. This was embarrassing. Still, she nodded her head. She didn't want to lie to him. She had enough secrets from everyone else.

He took her hands in his solemnly. "Lucy Banks. I assure you that I very much want to kiss you."

She was silent.

"Of course, if you don't want to kiss me," Harrison said, "I can understand. In fact, then I apologize for my forwardness."

She stared at him.

"Forget what those women said. They enjoy being cruel. You were their nearest target, that's all."

"They didn't think we were an appropriate match," she said.

"Well, I happen to think we're a very appropriate match."

"Indeed?"

He nodded solemnly.

"Because I'm an heiress, and you're a duke?"

A strange expression passed over his face, and he scrunched his lips together.

"That's not important," he said finally. "Because you are you. You are brave and kind and beautiful. Not every woman would have climbed into my library window solely to help their sister."

Her heartbeat quickened. He wasn't supposed to declare his affection for her. He wasn't supposed to proclaim a desire to kiss her.

But that was precisely what he was doing.

"I think," he said, "that it might be good to not think."

She raised her eyebrows.

"Thinking is good, but not always preferable."

"What is preferable?"

Harrison grinned salaciously, and her heartbeat quickened. Then, there was much more kissing.

CHAPTER TWELVE

Harrison ignored the faint disappointment when he did not see Lucy and her sister at the Serpentine the following day. No doubt, they could not perpetually sneak from their townhouse, maid in tow.

Harrison focused on rowing.

"Who's that person?" Sir Augustus asked.

Harrison's heart quickened, and he jerked his head to the side. Was it Lucy?

Instead, a man was pacing the edge of the Serpentine.

"Don't tell me one of the princes complained about our presence," Sir Augustus groaned.

The other rowers murmured mournfully behind.

"Isn't that person one of your mother's footmen?" Benedict asked.

Harrison wrinkled his brow. "You're correct."

"I think he's waiting for you."

Harrison scrunched his lips together. The duchess had never sent someone to speak with him before, but now it was clear that was precisely what she'd done.

The footman rushed toward Harrison, letter in hand. "I have a message for you."

Harrison took the letter reluctantly.

"And—er—I am supposed to verbally inform you that you are to visit your mother at once." The footman's face reddened, obviously uncomfortable with the task.

Harrison didn't blame the footman for being embarrassed: he was awfully mortified as well.

His friends chuckled behind him.

"I'll—er—just read the letter," he told the footman. Harrison unfolded the letter and scanned the words written in the duchess's clear, perfectly formed script.

Dear Harrison:
I demand to see you at once for tea.

He crumpled the missive. "I'll be there."

The footman shot him a relieved smile, evidently dreading the potential for the duchess's disappointment were he to fail to bring Harrison.

"Don't you always visit your mother's townhouse?" one of his friends asked.

"She wanted me to join her for tea," Harrison said, forcing a bland smile on his face.

His friends appeared unconvinced, but Harrison held his head high as he left Hyde Park.

Finally, he arrived in Grosvenor Square. He ignored the temptation to simply call upon Lucy.

The butler led Harrison into the drawing room. It remained decorated as it had in the last century, filled with pale pink damask wallpaper, gilt furniture, and cloud-filled paintings of wealthy people picnicking, the latter images similar to those that had inspired peasants on the other side of the English Channel to destroy their country.

The duchess was seated in an armchair. Despite the care with which the armchair had doubtless been created, her back remained straight. Relaxing was not something she allowed herself to do, even when sitting.

"Mother." Harrison bowed.

The duchess inclined her head. "Welcome."

"I hear we are having tea," Harrison said.

"We have much to discuss."

Harrison's heart tumbled.

"You've been spending much time with that Banks woman, haven't you?"

"Yes, I have." Harrison jutted out his chin.

"According to *Matchmaking for Wallflowers* you are as much as betrothed with Miss Lucy Banks. I thought it was a rumor, created by her indecorous parents, but after last night, I'm not certain."

"You shouldn't refer to her parents like that."

The duchess's gaze narrowed, though it did not lessen the intensity of her icy eyes. "I don't know what you're doing with her."

"I'm having a good time. You must remember that."

"Of course," she said, her face rigid.

Harrison's heart hurt.

She would have been happier if his father had treated her better. He knew that. She had loved his father, and he'd betrayed her. Was it any wonder she was suspicious now? Was it any wonder she was cold and frosty and guarded?

It wasn't.

Harrison mustn't complain, not to an older woman who had suffered for years. He'd gained so much from her.

"You must be careful, my child. Obviously, you haven't forgotten."

"Of course, I haven't." He stiffened. Some things were impossible to forget.

"After all, Miss Banks's best friend was Princess Aria, and she had a disastrous wedding..."

"I remember," Harrison said.

"The point is," the duchess continued, "that it's quite likely they will be very careful with the banns."

"Yes," he said.

"And you know what would happen?"

"I do.".

She nodded, evidently appeased. "The benefits are immense. You must never forget."

"I haven't."

"Now that that's all settled," she said brightly, "let's have tea."

The last thing Harrison wanted was tea. He suspected it would come with scones and various afternoon delights he had absolutely no desire to eat. His throat felt dry. Still, it was difficult to go against her. It always had been.

She waved her hand in a regal manner, and a footman wearing his customary white wig and breeches, as if he'd wandered in from the court of King George III, hastened to them.

"Please," the duchess said in a regal manner, "inform the housekeeper that we would like our tea now."

"Yes, Your Grace." The footman swept into a deep bow.

The duchess murmured approvingly, perhaps pleased at the right angle he formed. Shortly after, the housekeeper bustled in carrying a platter. The silver tea service gleamed on top.

"Where would you like to have it, Your Grace?" the housekeeper asked.

"By the window, my dear. It is good to see out sometimes." She glanced at Harrison. "Particularly when one cannot depend on the quality of the conversation."

The housekeeper shot Harrison a sympathetic look, and he forced his face to remain solemn. He didn't want the housekeeper's sympathy. He didn't want anyone's sympathy.

The housekeeper and footman moved a small round table to the bay window that overlooked Grosvenor Square. They carried the duchess's favorite teal upholstered armchairs, which were adorned with long strips of gold, to the table. The gilded furniture matched the gilded candelabras that perched on various sideboards, as well as the piano. The whole place sparkled and shone. No wonder the duchess never desired to leave this house and all its pleasures.

"Perhaps we can talk about something else," he said.

"Then your mind is not utterly occupied with thoughts of that redheaded girl?" the duchess asked.

"My mind is filled with many things," he said lightly.

"The estate, perhaps?"

"Ah, yes."

The duchess nodded approvingly. "You always excelled at handling that."

He nodded and formed a smile with his lips, but for some reason, the movement seemed stranger than before, as if it were physically difficult.

"Isn't my son so wonderful for visiting me?" the duchess cooed to the housekeeper.

The housekeeper nodded rapidly. "Oh, yes, Your Grace. He's a fine young man. You must be very proud."

"I am." The duchess stared at him. "He does nothing to disappoint me."

"How nice," the housekeeper said.

"He knows at my age and with my heart that such a thing could be disastrous."

The housekeeper's eyebrows shot up in a startled manner as she continued to place the tea service on the table.

"He is a sweet boy," the duchess continued. "He always has been."

Harrison gave a tight smile. Pretending was becoming more and more difficult.

CHAPTER THIRTEEN

Isabella sauntered into Lucy's bedroom and clasped her hands together. "I knew it! You only had to put your mind to it, and you found yourself a suitor."

Lucy swallowed hard. She'd never lied to her sister before and she had no urge to start.

"And you couldn't have found a more dashing suitor." Isabella plopped onto Lucy's bed. "Sturbridge is ever so handsome."

"That's what everyone says."

"And he wouldn't be friends with darling Benedict if he weren't also kind. Benedict speaks most highly of him."

"How nice." Lucy's lips wobbled, and for a moment, she wondered what it would be like if Harrison truly was courting her.

"Just think!" Isabella exclaimed, and her blonde curls bounced. "We could have a double wedding."

"A double wedding?" Lucy murmured faintly, and her stomach tightened.

Isabella nodded her head rapidly. "It would be ever so much fun. Two best friends marrying two sisters."

The pain in her stomach intensified, and she averted her gaze in as casual a manner as possible. "We haven't reached the marriage stage yet."

"Of course." Isabella waved her hand nonchalantly. "But I've seen the manner in which you two look at each other. It's only a matter of time before Sturbridge comes lugging some heirloom stone over here and pronouncing an urge to live happily ever after with you."

"You're overly romantic."

"I'm not the one dancing in his arms and receiving his calls. Benedict assured me the duke must be truly smitten." Isabella leaned conspiratorially toward her. "Even his mother is taking the matter seriously. It seems that Sturbridge has never acted this way with anyone before. And you know what that means?"

"What?" Lucy asked faintly.

"It means, dearest sister, that you're the one for him."

Lucy's mouth dried. Isabella's blue eyes sparkled with even more than their customary force. The Mediterranean Sea seemed to be shimmering right inside her eyes. It was a wonder no painter had dragged her outside to do her portrait.

But she couldn't let Isabella think she was on the verge of marriage. She couldn't pretend. Not with her.

"There's something I need to tell you." Lucy's voice wobbled.

A wide smile burst onto Isabella's already adorable face. "Don't tell me you're already betrothed!"

Lucy swallowed hard. Telling Isabella the truth would be even more difficult than she'd anticipated.

"Benedict said that you wouldn't get engaged until the summer," Isabella chattered happily. "But *I* said it would be even quicker." Isabella grinned. "Benedict proposed to me the third time we danced."

"You mean you're betrothed?" Lucy's eyes widened.

Isabella tossed her head. "Of course not. He has to get permission from our parents first. I wasn't going to become secretly betrothed to him. Some women might like the idea of eloping to Gretna Green, but personally, I've always wanted a large wedding. Besides, I don't like keeping secrets from people. Having a secret suitor is sufficiently secretive."

Isabella giggled happily, and guilt surged through Lucy.

"I don't like having secrets either," Lucy said. "Which is why I need to tell you something."

Isabella looked expectantly at her, but Lucy's throat dried, and her tongue suddenly forgot how to work. She coughed. "The truth is..."

"Yes?"

"The truth is," Lucy continued hastily, "Harrison is not really courting me."

Isabella's eyes widened. "Of course, he is. I saw him. *Many* times."

"Yes," Lucy said. "But he's not pursuing me in a romantic sense."

"You mean he hasn't confessed his love for you yet," Isabella said matter-of-factly. "Perhaps he's shyer than I thought. But I suppose that isn't completely surprising, especially since Benedict told me he's never courted anyone before. I wouldn't worry about that. He'll find the words. You can always gift him a book of poetry to help him along too. Shakespeare might be a bit cliched, but his sonnets truly are surprisingly effective. And if you think he would like something more modern, there's always Keats and Byron. He might even know Byron from Parliament."

"I offered to pay him to court me," Lucy blurted.

Isabella's eyes widened, and she halted speaking. The ticking of the grandfather clock in the next room seemed suddenly far stronger, as did the rustling of leaves outside.

"Truly?" Isabella breathed, and the pink glow on her face drained. She looked suddenly more fragile, as if she might shatter.

Lucy nodded. "He's doing it for Benedict. And he said it benefits him too, though he probably was just being a gentleman when he said that."

Isabella bit her lip.

"That's why he came to make certain that our social calendars were similar. It wasn't so that he could have the pleasure of my company. It was to make certain other people saw us together and...assumed."

"Like I did?"

Lucy nodded miserably.

"How did you plan that?" Isabella asked.

"I crawled through his library window and asked him."

Isabella's eyes widened further. "You didn't."

Lucy nodded, then giggled. "I did! You should have seen his face."

Isabella laughed, but then her face sobered. "You shouldn't have done that."

Lucy avoided Isabella's gaze. She wasn't used to seeing her sister's eyes be so filled with concern. "I did what I had to do. You're right. It's not fair that you can't be with Benedict unless I'm being courted. Harrison agrees."

"Harrison?" Isabella raised an eyebrow.

Lucy's cheeks warmed. "We've grown closer." She jerked her head toward Isabella. "But that doesn't mean he's anything besides my faux suitor."

"You mean you don't love him?" Isabella asked.

Love.

How odd that a word that contained only a single syllable should feel so heavy and unutterable.

Lucy drew back. Did she *love* him? For an odd moment, her heart quaked. But then she remembered she couldn't possibly love him.

"It's a business arrangement," Lucy explained. She straightened her torso. Perhaps, when she was sitting more upright, her heart would no longer quiver oddly. "Papa has many business arrangements. All completely impersonal."

"He doesn't have any business arrangements like you have."

"Well." Lucy shrugged and smoothed her dress. "The situation is different. Everything is pretend."

"I saw you exit the balcony with him last night," Isabella said, and her brow remained furrowed.

The room suddenly heated. For a moment, Lucy imagined being back at the ball, back on the balcony, back in the duke's sturdy arms. Heavens, she'd been able to feel every contour of his muscular chest. Her lashes swooped downward, and everything was dark, save the memory of the duke's lips on hers.

"Lucy?"

Lucy's eyes shot open. Isabella's gaze remained on her.

"I wanted to avoid speaking with Lady Letitia."

"No moonlight seduction?"

Lucy's cheeks heated.

"Something did happen," Isabella exclaimed.

"A few kisses," Lucy admitted.

"He kissed you?" Isabella's eyes widened. "And multiple times?"

Lucy gave an embarrassed nod.

"While I was attempting to make conversation with his dreadful mother, you were dancing in his arms and kissing him?"

Lucy grinned guiltily. "But it didn't mean anything. It was just because Lady Letitia was suspicious. That's all. So business!"

The last word was said at a higher pitch than normal. Lucy's throat dried. Apparently, talking about Harrison made her forget where her vocal cords were.

"I see." Isabella nodded slowly. "That can't be easy."

"It's fine." Lucy forced a smile on her face. "Harrison and I are friends. What better thing is that?"

"If you're certain..."

"Yes," Lucy said quickly. "I am." She hesitated. "I would appreciate it if you refrained from telling anyone. Not even Benedict."

"Benedict is the duke's best friend."

"Then the duke can tell him if he cares to do so."

"You're right," Isabella said reluctantly. "I'll be discreet."

Lucy nodded, and her shoulders eased. "I don't want to worry you. I just—"

"Don't want me to imagine a baby Harrison tottering around?"

"Precisely," Lucy said.

"Then I won't do that." Isabella squeezed her hands. "And thank you."

Lucy nodded. "Let's speak of something else."

"Very well." Isabella changed the conversation to some musings over the latest Parisian fashion and her overall sadness that designers no longer desired to drape their customers in fabric so they resembled goddesses.

Lucy made the appropriate expressions of sorrow, but her mind was preoccupied. Lately, Harrison was the only thing on her mind.

It would be difficult when the season ended, and she no longer saw him.

HARRISON MARCHED FROM the townhouse, fueled by milky Darjeeling tea and scones. He turned abruptly, then strode up the short flight of steps to Lucy's townhouse. In the corner of his eye, a lace curtain flickered. The duchess had seen him.

Well, he didn't care.

He wanted to see Lucy, even if the action was not condoned.

He knocked on the door and was ushered into Lucy's family's drawing room.

"Your Grace!" Mrs. Banks bounced up, and a smile played upon her lips. "What a lovely surprise."

Lucy shot him a startled look. No doubt she remembered that Harrison had agreed to call on her family once a week. Since he'd called on her yesterday and the day before, his presence was hardly essential.

For a moment, he worried he'd interrupted her. Perhaps she preferred tackling her knitting without his presence. But her lips spread slowly into a broad smile, and his heart clutched.

Heavens, she glowed.

How odd to think she'd been here so many months before, and he'd never even noticed her. Her skin had taken on a delightful peach blush that thankfully did not hide the adorable freckles scattered generously across her face.

Her eyes sparkled, and his gaze fell to her lips. He averted his eyes. He should never have looked at her lips. Now the only thing he could think about was how they might taste if he pressed his lips against her own.

He wanted to do just that very, very badly. He needed to taste them. It was a simple act of scientific curiosity, he told himself, absolutely nothing more. After all, he'd never kissed a redheaded woman.

"I wanted to invite you to my home in Cornwall," Harrison said. "It's fairly far away, but it is a wonderful summer destination."

Mrs. Banks glanced at her husband. "What do you think?"

Harrison had invited other people to his house party, but somehow, it seemed particularly important that they accept.

"Thornridge Castle is near the ocean," Harrison said.

"Did you hear that, Mr. Banks!" Mrs. Banks exclaimed. "The duke has his own castle."

Harrison gave a modest shrug. "It was built a long time ago."

He didn't want them to think he went about spending vast amounts of money on faux crenelated manor houses.

"And it's historical," Mrs. Banks squealed and clapped her hands.

"There are lots of corners in castles," Mr. Banks said. "I hope you do not intend to take my daughter to one of them."

"Papa!" Lucy exclaimed in an anguished tone, and her face reddened. "You mustn't speak to the duke like that. He's a perfect gentleman."

Harrison nodded, because it was the proper thing to do, but he didn't feel precisely like a gentleman now. Taking Lucy to a private place seemed like a most intriguing thing to do.

For a moment, he allowed himself to imagine stripping her of her clothes. He imagined kissing her skin. He shifted his legs hastily, conscious of Mr. Banks' gaze.

"I think that would be wonderful," Mrs. Banks declared. "We want to see as much of the country as possible."

"There will be some other guests, of course," Harrison said. "My friend Lord Brooke and some local gentry always come. The Duke and Duchess of Framingham are still in Sweden unfortunately, otherwise they would attend. They plan to arrive in London a few days after the house party begins. The Duke and Duchess of Sandridge will be present though."

"Ah. The chair falling fellow," Mr. Banks said. "I've heard about him."

"Er—yes."

"Did you say that the house party is in two months?" Mr. Banks asked.

"Yes." Harrison frowned. "I trust you won't be returning to New York before then?"

"No, no." Mr. Banks waved his hand, as if the idea were absurd and were to be brushed away. "But I know two months can be a long time for young people."

Lucy stiffened, and her eyes no longer met his.

Harrison sighed. Did Mr. Banks mean to imply he found it difficult to imagine he would still be interested in his daughter in two months? Was he so incredulous Harrison might find Lucy utterly appealing?

Mr. Banks didn't know about the plan Lucy and he had concocted, and the fact remained that Lucy was beautiful, caring and intelligent. He would be lucky to have someone like her in his life. It was absurd no one else had noticed that before.

"I assure you I will still very much want to have the pleasure of Lucy's company—and yours, of course—in two months. I am not fickle." His voice was sterner than he'd intended it to be, and he flushed.

Mr. Banks smiled pleasantly, though. "In that case, we would be most honored to join you."

Harrison's shoulders lowered. He hadn't even realized they were tense. He glanced at Lucy, and his heart warmed. Somehow, his heart always warmed when he saw her, as if it were confusing her with a fireplace.

"Indeed." Harrison shifted his legs, then rose. "Lucy, would you like to go for a carriage ride with me?"

Lucy's sister gave a broad smile and nudged Lucy.

"I-I suppose so," Lucy stammered, and Harrison beamed. Lately, he was also always beaming.

"Have a good time," Isabella said.

Harrison extended his hand to Lucy, and she took it. Energy pulsated through him at her very touch, and his next step was less graceful.

For some reason, her parents were smiling. Evidently, elegance was not highly prized in New York.

Harrison led Lucy to his carriage, thankful he'd decided to take it. He assisted her into it, spoke to the driver, then sat opposite her.

The carriage ride was short.

"We're here," Harrison announced as the carriage slowed. They needed to walk the rest of the way.

CHAPTER FOURTEEN

"This is the Serpentine." Lucy's eyes widened.

Harrison smirked. "I'm glad you took the time to remember the names of the London locations you visited."

"I knew it before."

Harrison's eyes glimmered. "Are you bragging?"

Lucy laughed and threw a silk throw pillow at him. "You know what I mean."

Harrison caught the pillow. "Pillow throwing is not an essential part of the courtship process."

Lucy narrowed her eyes. "Perhaps not all suitors need pillows to be thrown at them."

A few elderly matrons stared at them, halting their already minuscule pace to observe.

"I don't think they would agree with the necessity of pillow throwing," Harrison said, gliding his head toward the well-dressed women, their gray hair covered by fruit-and-feather adorned bonnets.

"Clearly, they haven't spent a long time speaking with you."

She extended her hand, and Harrison helped her from the carriage.

"To think I was your first-choice faux suitor," Harrison grumbled.

"I never told you that. You assumed."

"There's someone else?" Harrison raised his eyebrows. He scoured Hyde Park, as if half-expecting to see a more dashing, first-choice pick.

The idea unsettled him. He didn't want to imagine Lucy climbing into any other man's library and he didn't want to imagine any other man disappointing her. It was dreadful enough he'd done that to begin with.

"You were my first choice," Lucy murmured. The alto sound of her voice soothed him, and he stared at her.

Her green eyes glimmered, and sunlight played over the strands of her red hair. Her skin had a dewy sheen to it, a fact no doubt helped by the warm day. He'd never quite appreciated how many freckles dotted her delightfully sloped nose and her apple cheeks. He had a distinct urge to count them. Or at least trace them with his fingers.

"You're beautiful," he murmured.

Her eyes widened, and her long lashes fluttered over her eyes for a moment.

The air thickened, as if they'd landed in the Caribbean.

"You needn't say that," she said finally. "I-I don't think anyone can hear you."

He frowned. "You can hear me."

She nodded but seemed quieter than before. The rest of the throw pillows remained firmly on Lucy's seat.

Most women expected him to praise their beauty. Though he'd given his compliments on the overall symmetry of their features and overall loveliness of their attire, the compliments had always felt forced.

Lucy's beauty was less artfully concocted. Was it possible she didn't hear many compliments on her appearance? Perhaps people were always praising her sister. He felt guilty he had once considered her the less beautiful sibling.

He proffered his arm, and as she placed her fingers on the crook of his elbow, a jolt of energy moved through him. It didn't matter that he was wearing one of those thick tweed tailcoats his valet was always setting aside for daytime activities. Had Fletcher heard the stories of his sickly childhood? It didn't matter that Lucy's own fingers were enclosed in some Parisian gloves that managed to involve both flounces and ribbons, despite their small size.

The Serpentine glittered before them. The color was a darker blue than this morning, no doubt assisted by the now azure sky. Birds chirped, and butterflies flitted past them on their way to some new and interesting flower.

"Why did you take me here?" Lucy asked.

"I thought a woman who goes to the Serpentine at half six in the morning must be a true Serpentine enthusiast. Or was there another reason you went?"

Lucy's cheeks pinkened, and though the color was most charming on her, he felt a wave of regret. He didn't want her to feel any discomfort.

"It's also an excellent location for a couple to be seen," Harrison said. "Just in case people at a ball don't take sufficient note of our dances at a ball."

Lucy nodded, evidently appeased. "You are an excellent faux suitor."

"I know," he said, but for an instant, he imagined what it would be like if he were an actual suitor who was finding activities they would both enjoy and that would take her away from her family.

He swallowed hard. There were many reasons he could not dwell on the possibility of actual courtship. Besides, Lucy had already made it clear that she preferred to keep things businesslike.

"People are looking at us," Lucy murmured. "I think that's your friend, Sir Augustus."

Harrison grimaced. Sir Augustus was a good rowing partner, somebody who didn't mind the early hours at which other men scoffed, but he wasn't certain he could consider him a friend.

Sir Augustus seemed uncomfortable at times with Harrison's lofty title. Harrison gave a wry smile. At least that they had in common.

"There are some smaller rowboats here," Harrison said. "I thought I could take you on the Serpentine, if you find that enjoyable."

Lucy's eyes widened.

"Though some people aren't fond of being on boats," Harrison said quickly. "So, of course, if you fall into that type of people, we can just stroll the perimeter."

"No. A boat ride is an excellent idea."

He nodded. "Perhaps more people would notice us."

"Yes," Lucy agreed. "Though I'm personally quite fond of boat rides as well."

He turned to her. "You are?"

She nodded. "I sometimes traveled by boat to my friends' summer houses in Long Island and Newport. Isabella sometimes got seasick, but I always enjoyed the journey. Water is so peaceful. It seems impossible to worry when one is on it. Provided, of course, that one is not worried about drowning."

Harrison grinned. "I promise not to topple us into the Serpentine."

He paid the boatman and assisted her into a boat. Then he followed her into the boat and took hold of the oars.

She smoothed her dress, but she didn't need to do that. She was already beautiful. His heartbeat quickened for some reason. No doubt his heartbeat was pitter pattering at an unusual rate because of the exertion of getting into the boat, and it wasn't because he was actually feeling romantic. Perhaps his heart had never caused him any trouble, but older people were always clutching their heart, and he had had a birthday two months ago. Any other reason was impossible.

He'd vowed long ago that romance was not something he would pursue. Perhaps after the duchess died, things might be different. But then, he wouldn't be on a boat with Lucy Banks.

He bit his lip. He didn't need to think about that now. Unlike Harrison's father, ill-health had never plagued the duchess.

"You must have spent some time on the sea as a child," Lucy said.

Contentment swept over his face. "Cornwall is beautiful in the summer. The estate borders the ocean.

"Where in Cornwall is it located?"

"Near Tintagel." He leaned nearer her. "That's where King Arthur is rumored to have lived."

"Ah." Her eyes sparkled. "As the nearest aristocrat in that region, perhaps you are a descendent of King Arthur's."

He swallowed hard. "That w-would make sense."

She gave him an odd look. One problem with Lucy was that she was very intelligent. She was her father's daughter.

"Is there a reason you have reservations?" she asked.

There was the question. This was the time he could tell her everything. He could share his secret, and perhaps because they already shared a secret, he trusted she would keep his.

In fact, he had the definite sense it might be nice to share everything with her. It would be nice to discuss it with someone besides the duchess. She might even understand.

He shook his head.

The idea was absurd. Lucy had come to him for a business arrangement. She hadn't come to learn about his past. He shouldn't even have entertained the thought in his mind, however momentarily.

Suddenly, the privacy of the boat seemed unwelcome. If they'd simply strolled the Serpentine, he wouldn't have become tempted to tell her everything. He would have been too conscious of the fact they could have been overheard.

He cleared his throat. "I only meant I don't believe in fairytales."

"You don't believe King Arthur existed," she said, but disappointment flitted over her face.

Perhaps she'd suspected he had had more to say. Perhaps she knew him already. How had she managed to know him better already than Augustus? Or even Benedict?

But he knew he'd chosen Benedict and Augustus to be his friends for a reason. They were mostly good-natured, mostly up for adventure, and neither man was prone to rumination. Pondering things wasn't their favorite thing to do, at least when there were athletic activities to pursue and tailors to visit.

"One of the nice things about my estate is that it is on the north side of the county," Harrison said, suddenly finding the need to talk about anything, even geography.

"Indeed?" Lucy asked.

He nodded. "It's quieter. Fewer people sailing to France or the United States."

She raised an eyebrow.

"Not of course that it is bad if people do want to go to those countries," he said hastily, in what he hoped was a sufficiently gentlemanly manner.

She grinned. "Good."

Everything was fine again, and contentment flitted through him. He rowed methodically through the water, moving his oars in perfect rhythm. The sun shone behind Lucy, and she shimmered and sparkled.

LUCY PRETENDED IT WAS perfectly normal to be on a boat with a handsome, eligible duke. Judging from the stares of the passersby, not everyone was utterly convinced.

She sighed. She'd hoped leaving New York would have been able to give her a fresh start, and that people would forget.

She loved him.

Fiddlesticks.

Perhaps she'd always loved him. Perhaps that was why she'd blushed whenever he'd appeared at her parent's townhouse, and perhaps that was why she'd tried to avoid him, even when he was gallantly assisting her friend find happiness with Mr. Rupert Andrews.

Perhaps she'd always known her fate, even though she'd avoided it. And perhaps that was why she'd thought immediately of him when she required a faux fiancé.

Her heart rattled uncomfortably in her chest.

She shouldn't have done anything. All that she'd discovered was that Harrison was good and kind. It was better when she'd just thought him handsome. Then it had been easy to assign him entirely undeserving negative characteristics. She could tell herself that he was vile and self-important.

But in truth, Harrison was none of those things.

He was modest and uncomfortable with his title. He didn't talk at length about the accomplishments of his ancestors, as if to imply that if England were waging a brutal war now, that naturally, he would singlehandedly lead the country to victory.

He was understanding. Somehow, she hadn't thought he would be. Sometimes, she thought he knew her too well. He seemed to understand the exact dynamics of her and her family.

When he'd visited her parents, he hadn't rolled his eyes at her parents' propensity to exclaim and exaggerate. He hadn't told her father that he worked too much. On the contrary, he'd seemed to admire her father's position and had spoken more at length about it than anyone else in this country had done. Even people Papa's age had been mystified by his profession, declaring a personal preference for reading philosophical tomes, as if the mere fact gave him a heightened understanding of the universe, even though the people who indulged in such reading seemed the furthest away from the struggles of daily life.

Harrison never smirked because her parents had not attended a certain opera or because they took open delight in some music arrangements, a sign to others less of their sophisticated taste than an indication that they'd most likely never even heard the arrangements before.

He'd never sighed in a wearisome manner when Mama had fretted over food choices, even when Lucy herself had.

No, Harrison was different from most men. And the differences were good.

I won't fall in love. I won't fall in love. I won't fall in love.

Lucy scrunched her lips together as if the action might prevent the emotion from happening, even though she had the horrible sense that she'd fallen long ago.

Most likely, the action would only serve to make her slightly less attractive, a state that she couldn't fall into, given her already imperfect features.

No doubt, Isabella never scrunched her lips or furrowed her brows, even though she wasn't working with freckled skin or a shade of hair that had caused people long ago to liken the owners of it to witches and still made people offer, at best, sympathy.

She forced herself to chatter about the geography of Cornwall and not on Harrison's occasional melancholic glances and what they might mean.

CHAPTER FIFTEEN

The days turned into weeks, and finally, it was time to visit the duke at his manor house in Cornwall.

"We shouldn't be going to this place." Papa entered the carriage and clutched his briefcase to him.

"You enjoy the travel," Mama said. "We're making the most of our time in England. Besides, I expect a betrothal between the Duke of Sturbridge and our dear daughter, Lucy."

"I suppose that's a reason to go." Papa scooted further into the carriage so Mama could sit beside him.

"Not n-necessarily," Lucy stammered.

She didn't want her parents to be unhappy when they realized that the duke had never had marital plans for her.

"What nonsense," Mama said. "I know when a man is in love, and that man is in love."

Lucy and Isabella exchanged glances. Isabella shook her head slightly, and Lucy decided not to protest more.

This had been just what Lucy had wanted. Her parents believed the romance, and she was going with her family to the duke's house. Her sister had been secretly betrothed for the past week. No doubt they would soon announce their engagement, and Mama and Papa would exclaim that Isabella had beaten Lucy to it, but they wouldn't be that reproachful.

"Thank you," Isabella mouthed, and Lucy nodded.

It was of no concern. Well, almost of no concern. If it had been of absolutely no concern, her heart wouldn't ache when she thought about the duke, and her stomach wouldn't hurt when Mama and Papa talked about her impending happiness with him.

They didn't know it was impossible.

They didn't know she'd been lying this entire time.

Still, it was her plan, and it was going well. Sometimes, one had to think logically about matters. One had to come up with solutions that might seem unconventional to other people, but which led to fabulous, fantastic results. That's what Papa had always taught her about business, and she'd listened. This was going exactly according to plan.

Her heartbeat fluttered, even though she told herself it shouldn't and that it would be dreadful for her heart to make any such movements to imagine that it possibly belonged near Sturbridge and not right here with her family.

The carriage jerked to a start.

Lucy folded her hands in an appropriate manner. They wouldn't suspect. They mustn't suspect.

She stared out the window. The carriage developed some speed and the beautiful facades merged together. In an hour, they would exit London, and by next week, they would arrive at Thornridge Castle.

They stopped in quaint public houses and taverns for meals, and Mama insisted the driver also stop at every castle, hauling out their sketchbooks so they could record their journey.

Finally, after days of variable food and sleep, the carriage stopped, and she followed her parents from the carriage.

Thornridge Castle soared above her. She'd thought the duke's townhouse was grand, but this was no comparison. Beautifully arranged Grecian columns glistened under the sun. A fountain spurted up from a large, still, clear pool of water. Birds chirped with greater force than anywhere Lucy had ever seen. No doubt the duke's estate gardeners had brought them here specifically.

"Sturbridge must have a lot of money, indeed," Papa said.

"Almost as much as you, I warrant." Mrs. Banks craned her neck up.

"Perhaps so," Papa agreed. "Come girls, let's meet these British people."

They strolled toward the steps, then Lord Brooke exited the castle's large doors. A wide smile spread over his always cherubic face, and he descended the stairs.

"Lord Brooke is here," Mama said.

Isabella beamed. "Indeed he is."

He hurried down the steps, then stopped before Isabella. His blue eyes sparkled, and he swept into a deep bow. "Good afternoon."

"Good afternoon," Isabella echoed in response.

Papa frowned slightly.

"Let's go inside," Lucy said hastily before her parents became suspicious. They entered the foyer.

The duke exited from another room. His face lit up, and he hurried toward them. "Welcome!"

"We do have some guests already." He looked toward Aurora and Leticia. "Some people are very punctual."

"Some people are very eager to spend time with you," Lucy said, but her heart ached a bit. She knew Leticia and Aurora were astounded the duke had paid any attention to her. In their minds, it was utterly evident the duke should be paying attention to them.

Lucy understood why. Their parents had actual titles, not just money hastily scrambled together, albeit in significant sums, over the past two decades.

"Let me show you around, Miss Banks." He glanced at Lord Brooke. "I believe you can show the younger Miss Banks around?"

Lord Brooke beamed. "It will be my pleasure."

A cloud drifted over Papa's face. "Do we get a personal tour guide as well?"

Lucy's heart almost sank.

"Yes. We have an expert." Harrison gestured to an older woman wearing a black dress. "Come, Mrs. Howard."

The woman approached them.

"This is my housekeeper," Harrison said. "She'll show you around. She's lived here even longer than me."

"You were born here?"

"All Dukes of Sturbridge were born here." He exchanged a glance with the housekeeper, then Mama and Papa were whisked away.

She was alone with the duke and she liked it.

THE NEXT DAY, GUESTS filled the manor house. Though she'd happily strolled the estate with the duke yesterday, now uneasiness moved through her. His friends had arrived: the Duke and Duchess of Sandridge, the Duke and Duchess of Jevington, and the Duke and Duchess of Ainsworth. People thronged about them, and Lucy was reminded she was not part of the aristocracy and had been barely tolerated in the *ton*.

Her best Parisian day dress, white with red and green bows festooned on the hem, suddenly seemed fussy compared to the natural sophistication of the other women. The dress would have looked more becoming if the red ribbons had not clashed with her red hair.

Lord Brooke nodded at Isabella, and Isabella turned to her.

"I'll be fine," Lucy said. "Enjoy."

"You're the most wonderful sister." Isabella hurried away.

Lucy was alone. Letitia and Aurora were staring and giggling at her, and Lucy's stomach sank. They were talking about her. She knew it. Sometimes they'd talked about her at school. This was similar. She inched away, but the women made no effort to lower their voices, and she could hear them insulting her.

"She must be mad spending so much time with the duke, as if the duke could ever love someone like her," Letitia said.

"She's an idiot," Aurora said.

In the next moment, Harrison appeared. Fire had taken hold of him, and his whole face glowered. "Do you practice saying those comments in advance? Or is your mind naturally so vile?"

The women widened their eyes and glanced at each other. Suddenly, they looked far less confident and smug. One of them tucked a blonde ringlet behind her ear, even though her lady's maid probably would have advised her not to do that. Another one opened and closed her mouth as if she were playing a fish at the Christmas pantomime.

"I'm sorry," Aurora said finally. "I'm afraid that came out poorly."

"It came out horribly." Harrison's voice was low and deep and dangerous. "It came out dreadfully terribly."

Aurora managed to look ashamed. She hung her head, though not before surreptitiously scanning the room to see whether anyone noticed them. Perhaps she was ashamed at having offended a duke, or perhaps she was simply pleased to be speaking with a duke as long as their voices remained soft.

"It's fine," Lucy said finally. "We don't need to cause a scene."

"Everyone should know about these women's despicable behavior," Harrison said firmly, as if he were one of his ancestors from several centuries ago, urging his comrades to go and impale Frenchmen with swords and smash their heads with axes and maces.

Lady Letitia smirked.

"You mustn't do that," Lucy said. "Don't you see?"

He furrowed his brow and gave a slight shake of his head.

Lady Letitia's smirk widened.

"If you did that, everyone will know the insult."

"And they'll disprove of it," Harrison said.

Lucy arched an eyebrow, and the stoic expression on Harrison's face crumpled.

Evidently, he *did* see. He understood that if he were to do such a thing, Aurora and her friend would simply repeat the words, and some people, even if not his closest friends, would find it amusing and true. Most people might wonder at Harrison's sudden gallantry, and they might term him bewitched and wonder just how far New York was from Salem.

They might reproach Aurora and Letitia in public, but their eyes would glimmer, and their lips would twitch, and Aurora and Letitia would not be in the least discouraged to find a new recipient or keep pummeling Lucy with insults.

"Come, Miss Banks." Harrison shot another glower at the woman in question. "Let's leave this riff-raff."

Letitia's face whitened, and Aurora's eyes goggled.

"I'm sorry about the atrocious company." Harrison craned his neck and scrunched his features into another terrifying expression.

Lucy smiled despite herself.

Harrison led Lucy away. "I'm afraid I haven't fulfilled my hosting duties."

"Do hosting duties extend beyond scowling at mean-spirited guests?"

"Er—yes," Harrison said. "Though that's a special service I provide. Not every host provides that."

"I know," Lucy said softly.

Harrison frowned. "Though every host should."

"You aspire to be a good host?"

Harrison's frown deepened. "I *am* a good host." He opened the French doors, and cold air floated inside. "I think you require a tour outside."

"That might be scandalous, Your Grace. Besides, haven't your friends just arrived?"

"Yes. But they can partake of conversation and Cook's sweets by themselves." He sighed. "I was coming over to you so that you might meet them."

"Oh." She fluttered her eyelashes down.

Evidently, he hadn't forgotten her. Of course, he hadn't.

"I should have approached you. I just—"

He grinned. "Were you feeling somewhat shy, Miss Banks?"

She nodded.

"I have nice friends. But you can meet them later. I'm glad I managed to frighten the largest gossips." He pointed at Aurora and Letitia.

"They are spending a lot of time examining the banquet table," Lucy agreed.

"They don't want to make eye contact with us," Harrison said. "Cook's creations do deserve attention, though."

"I suppose it isn't too scandalous to be in a garden in the middle of daytime with you," Lucy said. "You are the host, after all."

"Yes, I have a duty to show you around." His eyes shimmered. "I can point out any hazards. Gnarly tree roots."

"Or crumbling walls."

He gave her a stern look. "There are no crumbling walls."

She swallowed back a smile. "Naturally."

He nodded curtly, then led her further into the garden. They passed dainty rose bushes and vibrant flowers, the colors calculated to suit the surrounding floral arrangements. They entered an herb garden, and the scent of lavender and thyme wafted about her.

"I love this place," she said.

"It must be very different from New York."

"New York has its advantages."

He nodded. "Someday, I would like to go there." A curious expression passed on his face. "Much further in the future, of course."

She nodded, conscious the action wasn't supposed to make her heart hurt but aware that it did so all the same.

"I mean, you would probably be happily married then," he said. "With—er—tiny tots crawling around."

"Or running," she said.

"Yes," he agreed hastily.

The air was suddenly hot, the temperature rising despite the consistent breeze and the relatively mild force of the sun.

The sun always seemed stronger in New York. Sometimes she forgot how far north England was. Still, now the sunbeams seemed to have no trouble casting their full attention on her, and she blinked into the bright light as the back of her neck continued to warm and warm and *warm*.

She wished Sturbridge did not find it so necessary to let her know he could never marry her. They'd already agreed on that. He didn't need to remind her.

"Have you been inside an English maze?" Sturbridge asked suddenly.

"No."

Sturbridge pointed to a deep green, immaculately maintained hedge. "Come."

Lucy followed him, even though she was certain hedges were more dangerous locations to be found wandering alone with a man than spice gardens that were overlooked by the main buildings of a manor house.

CHAPTER SIXTEEN

HARRISON SHOULDN'T bring Lucy here. Still, no one went into this maze. It had been built several centuries ago when such things were popular, but now the novelty of mazes had vanished. Most people favored wandering in gardens where they weren't surrounded by thick hedges designed to intimidate and test their intellect.

Still, no place exceeded this place in privacy, and Harrison had to speak to Lucy. He couldn't risk their conversation being interrupted by someone wandering around upstairs, and what he had to say to her couldn't be said in a corner of a drawing room where one could never be certain of the auditory powers of nearby festivity makers.

He marched through the maze, conscious of Lucy behind him. Tall yew hedges lined either side of him, but their woodsy scent could not equal that of Lucy's distracting jasmine scent. He wanted to turn around and kiss her, but that was another thing he mustn't do.

"What did you want to talk to me about?" Lucy asked, and Harrison swung around.

"I want you to know you're magnificent," Harrison said.

Her eyes widened.

"Spectacular," he added. "And you're more courageous than any of those women inside."

"That's what you dragged me here to tell me?" A smile played on her lips. He wanted to capture it with his mouth.

He nodded.

"That was kind of you."

"I wasn't trying to be kind."

She raised her eyebrows.

"I was trying to be correct," he emphasized. "There's a difference."

"Is being correct important to you?" she asked.

He started to nod, then halted. A funny expression must have passed over his face because Lucy stared at him oddly.

He averted his gaze. He didn't want her to guess. No one could know the secret. He'd held it for too long to start confessing.

Lucy approached him with a determined look on her face. Then, she wrapped her arms around his neck and gazed at him. She kissed his cheek, and cherubs sang. His blood heated.

"What was that for?" he asked.

Her luscious lips curved, and her eyes shimmered. "Your sweetness."

Poets always spoke about the beauty of emerald eyes. Harrison fully agreed. He lowered his head toward her.

Her lips were so near, so full and red, and they looked utterly and completely succulent. She drew back from him, but Harrison pulled her back toward him, lifting her from the ground.

Then, Harrison kissed her.

Truly kissed her.

He claimed her lips in a carnal impulse. The kiss smoldered. She melted into his arms and clung to him.

Her soft breasts pressed against his chest, and his arms found the delicious curve of her waist. He inhaled her jasmine scent.

Then, ever so gently, she kissed him back.

His heart thrummed and soared, and he was grateful for the multitude of his ribs, lest his heart decide to venture to the sky.

Nothing was impossible with Lucy.

His cock turned to stone. It longed to touch her wetness and to thrust inside her silky folds. It longed for her.

He longed for her.

She kissed him with a passion that made his heart lurch.

He'd kissed before, of course, but he'd always had the impression that those women had been appreciating his status and title and the overall ability of his features to meet the standards for handsomeness. A kiss with him was something amusing to tell the other widows, when they tired of disparaging the dresses of their least-liked acquaintances.

This was entirely different.

No woman knew him better than Lucy.

No person knew him better.

Standing was quickly becoming a ridiculous activity, one that might leave them vulnerable to being spotted by second and third floor viewing guests. He dipped her to the ground, thankful that Cornwall's skies had decided to withhold from raining.

Normally, the dirt path could hardly be termed comfortable, but with Lucy in his arms, it quickly surpassed any bed in the world. He rested her over him, so the dirt would not stain her dress. Her soft bosom sank against his chest, and he ran his hands through her glossy red hair. Some of the pins had come loose, and he marveled at the length of her glorious strands that swooped around the delicate arch of her smooth shoulders.

She raised her head and grinned.

He'd never seen such beauty.

Freckles dotted her nose and scattered her cheeks. Her emerald eyes sparkled in a manner that would entice even the most practiced jeweler. He pulled her back toward him and trailed open kisses along the silky skin of her neck.

She moaned, and her long dark lashes fluttered down. She made that delicious sound again with her throat: low and velvety and utterly enticing.

He wanted to explore every inch of her. He wanted to be inside her. He wanted... Well, he desired everything.

And I mustn't have anything.

Harrison halted his exploration of Lucy's luscious curved body with reluctance.

She opened her eyes slowly, and confusion fluttered on her face.

"We shouldn't do this," Harrison whispered,

"I know." Lucy's voice was small.

"We're not married, and I can't—" He closed his eyes, and shame moved over him. "I fear I have some things to tell you. Some...unpleasant things."

He grimaced and considered his past and his lies.

For a moment, Lucy was silent. Then she shook her head. "I don't want to hear unpleasant things."

"Excuse me."

She raised her chin. "You can tell me later, if you want." She chewed on her bottom lip. "But now I'd rather just continue."

"You would?" His voice was hoarse.

She nodded, and her lips twitched. "And I suggest we do not waste time."

Then there was more kissing.

Harrison lifted Lucy's dress. He wanted to give her more. His heart stopped as he saw her long legs.

"You were correct," he said.

"About what?"

"Your legs are fantastic."

She giggled. "My drawers cover them."

"I can still tell."

"You're a leg expert?"

"I have many talents." Harrison ran his fingers over her silky legs, noting their shapeliness. "That said, I think I should inspect them more thoroughly." He pulled on her drawers and slid them down.

Then he pressed kisses along her legs, claiming them.

A distracted moan came from Lucy, and he grinned. He wanted to give her everything. He reached to where her legs connected and delved his finger into the deeper recesses of her womanhood. His long fingers teased her secret bud, now delightfully plump, making her buck forward.

He continued to lazily move his fingers, enjoying the sounds of her writhing on the ground. Then, he kissed her petal-like interior.

HEAVENS.

This was—

Well, Lucy didn't have any words for it, but she didn't want it to stop. She never wanted it to stop.

Her core tingled and tightened and trembled. Harrison was touching her—*there*. And though Lucy was certain it shouldn't have felt so good, it felt...delightful.

Her heartbeat pattered at an ever-increasing pace. Desire moved through her. Harrison quickened his kisses. The world thrummed, then swelled, then exploded.

Her heart raced, finally slowing.

Harrison moved from his newfound position between her legs and collapsed beside her.

"My sweetheart," he said. "My lovely sweetheart."

She wrapped her arms around his neck and pulled him closer to her.

Harrison had been about to tell her something unpleasant, and she didn't want to hear anything unpleasant. Most likely, he wanted to tell her that his mother would never permit the marriage and for some unspeakable reason that he would never go against her. Perhaps even, he would tell her that he required a bride who would be better suited to life in high society and who would never be the subject of scorn by women such as Lady Letitia. No, this was a far better plan.

Harrison removed her fichu, and his eyes shimmered. He seemed to find joy in her cleavage and traced the curve of her exposed bosom. Then he moved his lips to her bosom, and another moan escaped from Lucy's mouth.

Something hard and firm pressed against her thigh, and she reached for it exploratively, marveling at the girth.

"You're much larger than statues," Lucy said.

Harrison chuckled. "I require multiple fig leaves."

Sweat dripped from Harrison's brow, and she brushed his hair aside.

Harrison bit his lip. "Would you like to—?"

He didn't say the next word, but she was certain she knew what he meant. "I want everything."

She nodded, and Harrison freed his instrument from his flaps. Lucy ran her fingers against his velvet shaft, wondering how the skin that enveloped it could be so silky, and the instrument itself so hard. Liquid oozed from the tip, and he shuddered as she touched it.

"Did it hurt?" Her heartbeat quickened.

He smiled. "Absolutely not. In fact, you can continue."

He held her hand about his shaft and moved it in a rhythmic motion. His hand was large and heavy against her own. They returned to kissing, and then, Harrison's breath quickened.

Then, Harrison grunted and collapsed beside her.

"That was..." He shook his head and smiled at her, then pulled her close to him. His heartbeat thumped against hers, and his breath remained erratic.

She sighed, enjoying the feel of his legs, of his torso, of his arms.

They continued to kiss, lightly now, without the earlier frantic energy. Happiness wafted over her.

Twigs crunched, and Lucy scrambled from Harrison's arms.

The footsteps thudded nearer. Harrison heard voices. Voices that sounded curiously American.

Blast.

Harrison hastily tucked in his shirt.

"Let me help you." He slipped her dress on over her shift.

"Lucy Alice Banks." Mrs. Banks's voice barreled toward them, as if she were an alto preparing to sing an aria at an opera house.

Horror moved through Harrison, and he stepped back.

Lucy covered her bare chest with her hands.

"Heavens!" Papa exclaimed. "What have you done to my daughter?"

"It's not what it looks like," Lucy said hastily.

"I've made two children," Mr. Banks said. "I understand these matters."

Harrison gazed at Mrs. Banks.

For some reason, she was smiling. Then she clapped her hands and beamed. "There will be a wedding."

"There can't be," Harrison said, his voice hoarse and his heart hurting.

"But you compromised her," Mr. Banks said. "She's ruined."

"Th-there won't be a baby," Harrison said meekly.

"Then she'll be ruined and alone." Mrs. Banks stared at Harrison in disbelief, then smiled. "But of course, you'll wed her."

Harrison was silent.

He didn't want to look at Lucy.

He didn't want to look at anyone.

Guilt moved through him. "I can never wed her."

Lucy scrambled up, then ran away.

CHAPTER SEVENTEEN

Lucy scampered from the garden, wishing they'd been anywhere else besides a maze. At one horrible point, she ran toward a dead-end and had to sheepishly hurry back, afraid someone would see her. *Heavens.* Her heart ached as if somebody were twisting it, turning it into some horrible knot.

Tears filled her eyes.

I won't cry. I won't cry. I won't cry.

But in the next moment, the whole world went blurry. In the moment after that, hot tears fell on her cheeks, and her nose erupted with liquid.

She pressed her handkerchief against her face, hoping for some semblance of respectability. None was to be found. There was only the sound of her hiccupping breaths.

This had been a terrible plan. She never should have succumbed to the sensation of having Harrison's arms about her. She should have known better. She *had* known better. And yet, when he'd sat near her and his dark brown eyes had bored into her, her heart had simply fluttered.

It had seemed impossible not to narrow the distance between them, not to marvel at the firmness of his sturdy chest, not to do anything else but kiss and kiss and kiss him.

Yet, when they'd been discovered, he'd been so quick to announce he could not marry her. All the love they'd shared together, all his insistences there was no one else he cared for, no one else he wanted to marry. No one else, even, that his mother was encouraging him to marry.

Despite all this, at the first prospect of a forced marriage, he'd pretended nothing had happened, even though everyone could see her bare bosom, flushed face, and tangled hair. Heavens, even *his* hair had been tangled.

He would rather let her be ruined. He'd rather let her destroy her reputation in the most permanent of all manners, would rather besmirch her, so people would think that not only had she been too available, but that she'd also not been sufficiently enticing.

Because if she had been enticing, wouldn't he have proposed? Wouldn't he have said he wanted to spend his life with her? Hadn't that happened to her other friends who'd made matches that everyone deemed impossible? But with her, despite her money, it hadn't happened.

Lucy slinked through the garden, avoiding the large windows that stared at her. She didn't want to imagine the people inside. Would they see her now, clutching a handkerchief, or would they hear about her later and think about her in amused tones?

Would they scoff that she'd imagined there could actually be something between her and Harrison, the Duke of Sturbridge? Would she serve as a warning symbol for other people about the importance of maintaining low expectations? When one hoped for more, even for a kiss with a man who was everything, only disaster could ensue.

Lucy's chest tightened, and she continued to blink. She cleared the wet tears from her face and pretended everything was perfectly normal and as it should be, even though it was a lie.

She gazed back at the maze. Heavens, they were still there. Were they still arguing with the duke? Was the duke still listing all the reasons he couldn't possibly marry her?

A sour taste invaded her throat.

This was supposed to be a pleasant weekend. It wasn't supposed to end in tears. She'd been so happy before, so utterly, completely naïve.

Leaves and twigs clung to her dress, remnants and reminders of the maze. She lowered her torso and strove to remove them. She squeezed her eyes and willed herself not to cry.

Finally, after she'd achieved some semblance of a twig-free dress, she raised her chin. Her heart felt like it had gone missing from her chest, but she proceeded inside the castle.

Lucy entered the house, thankful the butler was not waiting at this entrance. She hurried toward the stairs, hoping no one would see her.

Somebody opened the door behind her quickly, and footsteps thundered behind her. Her heart sank.

"Lucy Banks!" her father roared. "We're leaving this moment!"

Her throat dried, and she turned around. Her father surely hadn't just screamed, had he?

Yet, her father most definitely was here. And worse, his loud voice, which he'd never put on display before, had brought the attention of other people from the drawing room. Some stared at her with concerned looks on their faces, but most appeared amused. Their lips curled and their eyes glimmered, and a few whispered to one another.

"Very well," she said.

"But first, I've got to kill that duke." Papa looked around at the surrounding guests. Unlike her, he did not seem to view the sudden abundance of people as a problem. Instead, he beamed at them. "Say, does anyone have a gun?"

A few eyebrows darted up at the statement.

"Some of us were going hunting tomorrow," one man said cautiously. "We have guns."

A few other men nodded.

"Good. I'll need to borrow one," Papa said.

"Papa!" Lucy cried. "You mustn't speak like that. You must not harm the Duke of Sturbridge."

He shot her a disappointed look. "I don't *desire* to harm anyone, but the way this man treated you, it's inconceivable that I wouldn't try to punish him. Don't you understand?" He turned around. "Besides, I thought you British people did duels here."

"Not anymore," somebody said.

"Yes, it's outlawed," a man sighed.

"Oh." A sullen scowl marred Papa's normally staid face, then he jutted out his sizeable chin. "Never mind the law."

"I don't want you to fight," Lucy pleaded.

"I don't like to see you get hurt, honey."

She shut her eyes. If he didn't like seeing her get hurt, what was he doing now?

"That man was compromising you," Papa continued. "And then he refused to marry you."

"Mr. Banks!" Mama's voice bellowed as if she'd been performing in Covent Garden for years. "What are you discussing?"

Papa's face reddened. At least he knew he should be ashamed. "I was just asking for a gun."

Mrs. Banks scoured the faces of the people around them. She must have seen their looks of pity and amusement, and on some, sheer disgust.

Her family didn't belong here. They were the Americans. They were too coarse. They didn't have titles. They were tolerated at some social events, but they didn't truly belong.

Mama shot Lucy a stern look, then turned to her husband. "Mr. Banks, we should go upstairs."

Lucy's chest hurt. Mama was disappointed in her as well.

None of this would have happened had she not made that arrangement with the Duke of Sturbridge.

Mama would have been able to enjoy these house parties without everything being violently removed from her. She would simply have been a woman with two unmarried daughters in London, and that would have been enough.

Now though, she was foolish, and Lucy had made her that way. Lucy's heart shattered. She'd hurt people. She'd hurt her parents. She'd hurt her sister. After all, Isabella was planning to enter this society. If her parents ever gave Isabella permission to marry Lord Brooke, could she be accepted as his viscountess? She'd even hurt the Duke of Sturbridge. His reputation was also tarnished, perhaps not as much as hers, but surely it could hardly be a benefit to him that he'd been found in the maze with her.

Though some men prided themselves on being rogues and called rakes, that wasn't the case for all men. She doubted it had ever been the case for Harrison. The man was naturally kind, naturally cautious. He wasn't the type to boast about ruining a woman's life because he'd wanted to spend some time with her on a bed.

"There's something you should know about the duke." Lucy raised her voice.

Mama shot a worried glace around her. "We really shouldn't be having this conversation." "This isn't the place."

"This is exactly the place, since Papa insulted him in public."

Other guests leaned forward. Lucy was aware of how large their presence was in this room. Her heartbeat quickened, but not in a pleasant manner. It quickened as if she were running for her life. Unfortunately, there was no way for her to escape.

Still, she could rescue the duke, and she addressed the guests. "The Duke of Sturbridge is not at fault."

Leticia's eyes glanced at the grass stains on Lucy's dress, and Lucy covered them awkwardly with a hand.

"But he lured you," Mama said. "He made you think there was something between you. He made you think there was an understanding."

"No, he didn't," Lucy said.

"We all saw him. We all saw how he danced with you multiple times at balls. We all saw how he sat next to you. Why, he even went to Hyde Park with you."

"Yes," Lucy said. "I paid him to court me."

Mama stared at her with a horrified expression on her face, then she laughed and looked around nervously. "My dear child, you are so amusing." She turned to her husband. "And you are amusing as well. Let's go upstairs. It's time for a nap."

Lucy rolled her eyes. Mama hadn't demanded she take naps, even when she was a child. There was no reason she would do so now.

"No, this is important," Lucy said. "I paid him."

"You absolutely did not," the Duke of Sturbridge said in his tenor voice. Evidently, he'd entered the manor house after them.

She turned to him. Heavens! His mere presence was enough to turn her to liquid. For one moment, she remembered his hands on hers, his lips on hers, his chest pressed against hers, and her legs quivered. Even her fingers shook, as if her fingernails had suddenly become heavy.

They hadn't.

The Duke of Sturbridge's presence merely changed everything.

"You're correct," she amended. "I didn't pay because you already have money. But I offered to pay, and that's similar."

"So he took it on as charity work?" Leticia asked.

More people giggled.

Mama's face reddened, and she jerked Papa toward her. She marched him to the stairs, then grabbed hold of Lucy's hand and dragged her with a force Lucy did not know her mother possessed.

"That will be quite enough," Mama scolded her, once they left the staircase and the eyes of the *ton*. "I've never been so ashamed in my life."

"I just needed to rectify things," Lucy said.

"Some things cannot be rectified."

Unfortunately, Lucy agreed.

HARRISON WATCHED MRS. Banks drag Lucy and her husband up the stairs. Lucy's tall, slender body became slimmer and slimmer until she reached the top of the steps and hurried away.

"That was incredible," Leticia said dryly, then turned to him. "I'm so sorry. How awkward." Her tone was icy yet somehow understanding. Not too long ago, he'd criticized her, but now she seemed to think the behavior of the Banks family had vindicated her earlier actions.

Sir Augustus elbowed him and laughed. "You certainly made an impression on that woman, you rogue."

"I'm not happy."

Augustus's eyes glimmered. "It's not terrible."

They didn't understand. They considered it amusing. They didn't care he might have broken someone's heart or that he might have ruined someone. For them, it was a cause for laughter.

CHAPTER EIGHTEEN

HARRISON'S COACH BARRELED toward Grosvenor Square, rumbling past the leisurely paced chaises, more designed for being seen in than for actual transport. The coach stopped, and Harrison tumbled out.

"This might take a while," he told his driver. "Bring my bags to the club. I'm sure you want to rest."

His driver gave a relieved nod, and Harrison sprinted toward the Banks's townhouse.

If only Lucy's family hadn't disappeared so quickly. If only he'd been able to reach Lucy. Cornwall was far from London, and too late, he'd realized her family must have taken an entirely different route to the capital.

He knocked on the door, and the butler answered. A dismayed look appeared on the butler's face immediately. Evidently, he knew what had happened.

"I suggest you leave," the butler said in a low voice. "For your safety."

"Is that the duke?" Mr. Banks roared.

"Yes!" Harrison shouted.

Her family was home. Thank goodness.

"You should go," the butler whispered, but Harrison stood his ground. He needed to speak with Lucy. It was absolutely vital.

"She's not here," the butler said.

"Oh." Harrison's shoulders slumped. "Are you certain?"

The butler's gaze drifted to the side, but he nodded.

Harrison swallowed hard. "Well, please tell her I was here."

The butler gave a curt nod, and Harrison headed for his carriage.

"Young man!" A forceful voice called out after Harrison, and Harrison turned slowly.

Mr. Banks stood on the steps to his townhouse in Grosvenor Square.

Carriages continued to glide regally about the square, but a few passersby had halted their strolls and were staring at Mr. Banks. Their mouths parted, and their gazes jerked from Mr. Banks to Harrison as if they were observing a tennis match.

Harrison's stomach drained. Didn't the man know people could see them? Didn't he know he was creating the sort of delicious gossip Lucy would despise?

Mr. Banks threw his briefcase to the side and marched toward Harrison.

Harrison had begun to think the man's briefcase was a permanent appendage to his body, given he'd never seen them separated. The man marched toward him, and Harrison suddenly felt sympathy for the British officers who'd been stationed in the former colonies and who had discovered that the bland-faced lawyers, stout farmers, and committed family men were willing to fight and to fight with brutality.

He half-expected fiery American companions of Mr. Banks to drop from the chestnut trees that dotted Grosvenor Square.

"Come here, young man," Mr. Banks hollered. "I'm not finished with you!"

Harrison's stomach dropped, willing him to stay on the other side of the pavement. His knees trembled, as if someone had exchanged them for the legs of a newborn colt.

Still, he made his way to Mr. Banks, keeping his chin raised. He was not going to act weak. Not at all.

Some well-dressed passersby halted their parade of the square and nudged one another.

"Mr. Banks," Harrison said coolly. "I was surprised to learn you left my castle."

"What?" Mr. Banks thrust his eyebrows together in obvious perplexity. "You know very well why we left. Stop trying to be polite."

Harrison attempted to roll his eyes subtly, so Mr. Banks would be more discrete. He couldn't talk about Lucy in front of all these spectators.

"Focus on me, Duke!" Mr. Banks shouted.

Evidently, subtlety was not an art form Mr. Banks had mastered. No doubt, he found it less productive than finding stocks to purchase and building his wealth to an immense degree.

"We can discuss this inside," Harrison said.

"Inside?" Mr. Banks put his arms on his waist. "You're not going inside *my* townhouse, you disgraceful man! You utter venomous being! You huge disappointment."

Harrison glanced to his side. More people glanced toward them. Some of them cupped their hands over their mouths as if to hide their amusement. Given the amount of gleeful sparkling their eyes were doing, they evidently should not have bothered.

"You compromised my daughter!" Mr. Banks roared.

The crowd halted tittering and gazed at Harrison with open suspicion.

"I didn't," Harrison said miserably, glancing at the crowd.

"Her bosom was visible."

"You're going to marry my daughter," Mr. Banks said coolly, and it occurred to Harrison that Mr. Banks might be quite effective in meetings. No doubt, Mr. Banks was able to force mergers to happen. His habit of reading ledgers of various companies in no manner precluded any aggression.

"I-I can't," Harrison said finally.

Sweat beaded the back of Harrison's neck, even though typically he left perspiration incidents for visits to the south of France in the height of summer.

Mr. Banks's face turned purple, though Harrison doubted he'd consumed too many aubergines. His fists tightened together, and his eyes took on a steely edge.

"I mean," Harrison said, "it's—er—impossible."

"Nothing is impossible," Mr. Banks roared, as if he were one of those colonialists fighting off a slew of red-coated British officers wielding the fanciest rifles.

But it was impossible.

Harrison had . . . secrets.

Lucy would be better marrying any other man in the *ton*. Well, the reprehensible men would be unsuitable. The elderly men seeking their second wives after a sudden spurt of lust overtook them would be similarly inadequate. Even Sir Augustus, who was unattached, would be a miserable companion, despite his gifts at rowing. In fact, Harrison couldn't think of a man offhand to whom she would be suitable.

Still, it wasn't him.

He knew that.

She deserved everything in this world. She didn't deserve his secret. She didn't deserve to always pretend. And she certainly didn't deserve for any harm to come to their children. Because if people found out . . . He swallowed back a sour taste in his mouth. No, if people discovered the secret, there would be consequences. The sort of consequences that would prevent their children from ever being welcome in any club or ever securing a place at Eton or Rugby.

Harrison gazed about him, his eyes moving wildly. A crowd had formed around the doorstep. Some people he recognized. A few other women he did not immediately recognize, but their well-tailored dresses, adorned with an abundance of flounces and displaying oversized sleeves, despite the obvious expense of the fabric, spoke to bulging reticules.

A hack rumbled over the tilestones. The black carriage had never looked so appealing before.

"I'm sorry, I can't." Harrison bounded toward the hack.

"Stop!" Mr. Banks's voice barreled toward him with an even greater force than before, but it didn't matter. Mr. Banks had already revealed to various gossip enthusiasts that Lucy, darling Lucy, was compromised.

Nothing mattered now.

"Halt!" Harrison waved his arms at the hack.

"I have passengers," a gray-haired driver grumbled, staring at Harrison's glossy beaver-skin top hat with open distaste. Perhaps he was accustomed to self-important aristocrats demanding rides.

"Stop!" Mr. Banks voice sounded behind Harrison, and he glanced behind him. The man's voice sounded even louder than before. Mr. Banks ran down the pavement toward Harrison.

"I'll sit beside you," Harrison yelled, hurrying toward the hack.

"Nonsense," the hack driver said.

"Stop!" Mr. Banks shouted again.

Harrison hesitated, then quickly clambered up a horse, wondering how postilion drivers regularly did this.

"What are you doing?" the hack driver asked.

"Just riding postilion style," Harrison exclaimed. "I'll pay extra!"

The horses and carriage sped away, though Harrison's guilt only continued to grow.

"FAMILY DISCUSSION!" Papa's voice thundered from the foyer, and Isabella and Lucy exchanged glances.

Lucy and Isabella had been reading books in Lucy's room, though in Lucy's case, that had involved pretending to read, and in Isabella's case, that had involved murmuring sympathetic phrases.

"Come down!" Papa bellowed again. "Now!"

Right.

Lucy had definitely heard him. Family discussions weren't anything Papa had ever desired before. Papa had always been determined to spend his time at home reviewing his investments.

But then, from the furious tone of his voice, most likely, he did not desire mere chit-chat.

Lucy and Isabella scrambled to the corridor. They hurried past the dainty sideboards, heavy mirrors that only served to illuminate their creased attire and disheveled appearance, then finally down the stairs to the foyer.

Mama was already there, but given the unconventional tilt of her cap, Lucy suspected she'd also run.

"You should not yell, Mr. Banks," Mama said.

"This is an emergency."

Lucy and Isabella exchanged glances again. Had Papa received an unsettling letter from the United States delineating some tragedy?

"Did someone...die?" Isabella ventured finally, and her chin trembled.

"I suspect your father is referring to your sister's reputation. In fact, one could call it a death." Mama raised her chin. "I would call it a death."

Lucy swallowed hard. She'd apologized every day on the uncomfortable journey back to London.

"Your mother is correct," Papa said. "We must leave."

"Leave London?" Isabella's voice squeaked, and Lucy's heart thudded.

Isabella hadn't told their parents about her secret betrothal to Lord Brooke.

"Leave the British Isles," Papa said.

Lucy blinked.

"We can't stay here," Papa added.

Isabella, Mama and Lucy were silent.

"I don't want to go," Isabella said.

"We don't have to leave," Lucy said. "I-I don't mind staying."

"My word is final." Papa's voice was stern. "We leave tomorrow."

"Tomorrow?" Mama's eyes widened. "But that's—"

"In one day," Papa finished for her. "I suggest everyone pack."

CHAPTER NINETEEN

No message from Lucy had come, but the next day, Harrison returned.

"Your Grace." The butler shot him a shocked look.

"I am here to see Miss Lucy Banks and whatever chaperone she deems necessary in the drawing room."

"I see." Normally he would offer to take Harrison's coat. Instead, his expression seemed stiff, and his face took on an unusually pale color despite the fact most people in London already tended toward paleness. "I'm afraid that's impossible, Your Grace."

"Oh, is Miss Banks out again?" Harrison smiled. This was not terrible news. She was out. That might mean she was feeling better. And if she was feeling better, well, perhaps then he had not utterly destroyed her life.

"She is out," the butler said, "in the ocean."

Harrison's eyebrows darted up. "I don't understand."

Perhaps Lucy had wanted to take an excursion to see the Thames.

Harrison wouldn't call the Thames an ocean. It was obviously connected to the ocean though—perhaps the butler had simply exaggerated.

After all, butlers were prone to exaggerate both the importance of the guests who were visiting and the importance of the inhabitants themselves. Could it be any wonder that a butler might exaggerate the importance of the Thames and accord it ocean-like qualities?

Perhaps though, Lucy had visited Brighton or some other seaside location where she could appreciate the beauty of nature and come back in a fortnight.

Heavens—a fortnight was too long away. Hopefully, she would only be gone for two or three days.

He did want to see her again soon.

The butler's expression remained somber. "She is sailing for New York City."

"Oh." Sturbridge suddenly felt cold despite the fact the butler had not taken his frock coat and despite the fact there was no earthly reason for him to feel cold when the sun seemed intent on shining with even more than its normal force. Even the clouds had stayed away today.

"But that wasn't the plan. They were supposed to stay until September."

"No," the butler admitted. "Indeed not, Your Grace. It seems Miss Banks was determined to form a new plan."

"I see." Sturbridge raked a hand through his hair, and his top hat fell.

The butler bent to pick it up.

"I'm sorry."

"You look like you've had a shock, Your Grace. You're welcome to come into the drawing room. No one is there. Her—er—entire family is gone. We're just packing up. There will be new guests to rent it later, but I'm sure the housekeeper could prepare some tea or coffee to fortify you."

"I should leave and let you continue your preparations."

The butler gave him a tight smile, but his eyes remained worried. *Blast.* No doubt Harrison's pain was obvious. It didn't matter. Everyone could know he was devastated. He deserved it after what he'd done. He deserved all this pain.

"Do you know if they are returning to Grosvenor Square?" Harrison asked, even though the question was ridiculous. He knew they weren't returning. "Was there perhaps an urgent issue that required the attention of everyone in the family?"

"I think you know the urgent issue."

Harrison swallowed hard. "I see."

"I'm sorry, Your Grace. I think you were fond of Miss Lucy Banks."

"I was," Harrison said.

"I hope that you had some happy memories with her."

Harrison nodded and thrust his top hat onto his head with rather more force than the action required. No doubt, his valet would have to work extra hard to ensure it was not ruined. Then he swung around and marched back to his barouche. His heart pounded, and his steps faltered as if uncertain where he could place them.

She was gone.

She was gone his life and from all of London, all of England, all of Britain, all of Europe.

He gave a wry smile.

Well, Lucy never did anything in half measures. That was for certain.

He would never see her again. He would never speak with her across from the punch table. He would never waltz with her around the ballroom, conscious of everyone's stares.

He would miss her. He would miss her most awfully.

There was nothing he could do.

He imagined the ship moving faster and faster across the Atlantic, tearing her away from him forever.

He'd placed her in scandal. Perhaps in New York, she could rectify some of her reputation. Perhaps if they arrived home quickly, fewer rumors would have had the chance to reach New York and its high society.

It was for the best.

After all, he couldn't marry her. He hadn't realized when he accepted the Duchess of Sturbridge's request that he would be giving up all chances for love.

Harrison climbed into his barouche. The horses glided in their customary manner, waving their tails from side to side. A few people stared in wonder, just like they always did. It was a nice barouche, but he would prefer to have her.

Still, Lucy might be upset now, but in a few years, doubtless, she would be married and happy living a life with someone else. She wouldn't be burdened by his secret.

He returned to Robertson's Gentlemen's Club. The two guards nodded at him, just as they always did. He entered the club, quiet except for the sound of newspaper rustling as people turned the pages.

In truth, he had the money, certainly, to buy a larger townhouse. In fact, if he wanted to, he could buy the one Lucy and her family had abandoned. But it wouldn't be right to do so. He didn't like spending the money.

When he'd agreed to take on the role, it had been to be helpful. The duchess had insisted all the servants and she would be destroyed if a new family came to live at the castle. Since then, the true heir, some second cousin, had died. His son had also died in the war. Harrison wasn't certain who would come after in succession.

No, he absolutely refused to burden Lucy with his secret. How could he let her think he did not care? It wasn't true. He did care.

Harrison turned around abruptly and practically strode into Sir Seymour.

"Excuse me," Harrison said.

Sir Seymour's eyebrows lurched up. "Ah, want to get more alcohol? Well, I certainly understand."

"No," Harrison said. "I want something else entirely."

Sir Seymour bored his beady eyes into him, as if simply staring at Harrison would make him grasp Harrison's desire. On another day, the action might've made Harrison's lips twitch. Today, though, was different.

"I have the sudden urge to be on the water," Harrison said.

THE HORSES HURRIED through Grosvenor Square with rather more rapidity than normal. The carriage bounced.

"Speeding is unnecessary," Mama said.

"We are not missing that ship," Papa replied. "Besides, it will give you practice for the voyage. This is nothing compared to the Atlantic Ocean."

Isabella and Lucy groaned. Even Rose looked worried.

"The girls haven't forgotten," Papa said.

Even Mama's face appeared whiter than before, and she was wearing a fur coat over her pelisse and afternoon dress out of a suspicion of the ability of the porters to deliver their trunks to the ship correctly.

Isabella bit her lip and glanced out the window. Lucy followed her gaze. Would this be the last time she would see these elegant buildings? The last time she would be in London? Had she already seen Harrison for the last time?

She knew the answer though: of course, she'd never see him again.

She'd half-wondered whether he might dash to see her in London, but he had not. No doubt, he was in Cornwall now, merrymaking with his aristocratic friends as they made jests about her. Nausea moved up her throat.

She'd been anxious to return to New York and resentful her parents had dragged her here, but now she would miss London. She would miss *him*.

But of course, everything with him had been for pretend, and now everything was over.

"Halt! Halt!" A voice interrupted her thoughts.

Harrison.

He'd come for her.

Happiness surged through her, and she was conscious of the sound of horses' hooves following, then thudding beside the carriage.

"Halt!"

The voice didn't sound precisely like Harrison. Perhaps he'd sent a messenger. No doubt, he didn't know the exact route the carriage would take. He sometimes spoke of his valet, Fletcher. Perhaps this was him now.

But how had Harrison known to come for her? Why had he changed his mind?

The coach stopped, and her heartbeat quickened.

"What is this?" Papa's face reddened. "A common hijacking!"

"No one has asked for the coach, dear," Mama said reassuringly, but even her hands trembled.

"I suppose that's why people say to stay away from the East End," Papa blustered.

The door opened.

"I'm sorry, sir," the groom said, "but this man was most insistent. I thought perhaps it related to your work..."

"I'll speak with them. Don't worry." The man's voice was elegant, and his vowels were rounded in the most upper-class manner. This man was no common hijacker.

Unfortunately, this man was also not Harrison.

She knew that voice, and now that horses' trots were no longer masking his words, she recognized it.

"Benedict!" Isabella squealed.

Mama's lower lip toppled down.

"What's all this?" Papa barked.

In the next moment, Lord Brooke popped his head inside the carriage. His golden curls clung to his skin, which now had a velvety sheen. He beamed when he saw Isabella. "I got your message."

"Message!" Papa exclaimed. "What message?"

"I'm not going to let you leave London," Lord Brooke said. "I don't care what anyone says."

Isabella's eyes sparkled and shone.

"What's all this?" Papa asked. "We're in a hurry, young man."

Lord Brooke turned to him. His fingers shook, but he fisted his hands and jutted out his chin. "I love your daughter and plan to marry her."

Papa blinked. "You'll have to court her first."

Lord Brooke's face reddened. "I—er—am quite confident. I've been spending time with her, and—"

Papa's eyes goggled.

"Well, she told me last week that she would marry me."

"You did?" Mama breathed and jerked her head toward Isabella.

"Yes." Isabella nodded. "We're engaged."

"I don't want her to sail to the United States," Lord Brooke said solemnly. "I don't want to be without her for another second."

"But I haven't said yes!" Papa exclaimed.

"But Isabella has."

"And why didn't you tell us about this?" Mama asked.

"It was because I was unmarried," Lucy blurted. "And you had said that Isabella wasn't allowed to court anyone until I had a suitor."

"That's why you made that unspeakable arrangement with the duke?" Mama wrinkled her nose.

Lucy nodded.

"Well, Lucy isn't being courted now, so the rule still holds," Papa said. "And we're still late."

"I think—" Mama bit her lip and cast a sorrowful gaze at Lucy. "I think that Isabella should marry this Lord Brooke."

"Thank you, Mrs. Banks!" Lord Brooke beamed. "I'll look after her. I'll be the best husband in the world."

"But you said..." Papa wrinkled her brow.

"I don't think Lucy will ever marry after this scandal," Mama said. "So if Lord Brooke wants to marry Isabella, he can."

"Oh." Papa was momentarily silent.

Lucy's heart shuddered.

Mama was right. Who would have her now? And even though she didn't want to marry anyone, even though it seemed impossible to ever be close to anyone after Harrison, she didn't like that she didn't have any choices.

But this was what she'd known would happen. Isabella would marry Lord Brooke. That had sufficed as a happy ending for Lucy months ago, and it would have to suffice now.

"I'm delighted for you, Isabella," Lucy said.

"You are?" Isabella's eyes were dewy with tears. "I'd hoped Harrison might come for you too."

"You haven't seen Harrison?" Lord Brooke asked abruptly.

"No." Lucy's heart panged.

"Why?" Isabella asked. "Should she have seen him?"

Papa fiddled with the tassels on the curtain. No doubt, even he was embarrassed that Harrison hadn't tried to see Lucy.

"I just thought—" Lord Brooke shook his head. "I suppose not. It's—er—not important."

"Perhaps we can all stay in London?" Isabella asked.

"Nonsense. Your big sister is in disgrace. We're not having her presence impacting the start of your future life." Mama scrunched her lips together, then clapped her hands. "I have it! Rose, you must stay with Isabella."

Rose's eyes widened. "Indeed?"

"You like London, don't you?"

Rose nodded rapidly.

"Good," Mama said. "We must bring Isabella and you to a chaperone until the wedding." She scrunched her lips together. "I think the princess is in town. Let's go there."

Lord Brooke returned to his horse, and there was much celebration inside the carriage. But when Lucy closed her eyes, it was thoughts of Harrison, and not thoughts of Isabella's upcoming nuptials that occupied her mind.

CHAPTER TWENTY

Sir Seymour's mouth opened and closed as he stared at Harrison. Finally, he glowered. "The water? You want to gaze at the Thames? In Yorkshire, we have clear water, lake water. It's far improved."

"I don't doubt that," Harrison said. "In fact, I have more of a craving for the Atlantic."

"The Atlantic?" Sir Seymour's eyes sprang further up. "Surely, you mean the English Channel?"

"No." Harrison shook his head. "The Atlantic Ocean."

Sir Seymour's face paled. "You mean you intend to sail on that place with all the horrible storms?"

"Yes," Harrison said.

"With the wild waves?"

"Indeed."

"Where after weeks of travel, the only thing you reach is," Sir Seymour shuddered, "the former colonies?"

"They're called the United States now."

Sir Seymour covered his face with his hands. "Oh, heavens. You're already speaking like them."

This time, despite Harrison's sadness, his lips truly did twitch.

"But why would you do it? You don't need to."

"I would quite fancy it."

"But you're a duke. You're not some penniless peasant trying to make a new life."

Harrison swallowed hard.

"Are you to tell me you truly have an urge to visit that despicable country?" Sir Seymour pressed.

At least Sir Seymour had accepted the United States was its own country, Harrison supposed, but that had likely been a decades-long realization that was inconsistently acknowledged even now.

"It won't be too terrible," Harrison said. "Nice people, Americans."

Sir Seymour's jaw dropped open. "Nice people? They're loud. They're brash. They're used to long slabs of land with nothing in between." Sir Seymour leaned closer. "I think it makes them more used to screeching."

"I'm not worried about that."

"Cotton for your ears." Sir Seymour nodded. "Wise move, young man."

"There's something happening," one of the other older gentlemen said.

Sir Seymour stood and clasped his hands to his chest as if he were performing on a stage and found it essential for his melodramatic poses to be readily observed so even the most far-flung ticket holder would be able to get his money's worth.

Sir Seymour pointed his hand, now shaking, at Harrison. "This man intends to sail to America."

"No." The first gentleman clutched his heart.

A few others who had seemed deeply engrossed in their newspapers and books flung them to the side. Newspapers crumpled against one another, creating a cacophony of crunching sounds.

"He's probably jesting," a second gentleman said, eyeing Harrison. "He is young. Young men do jest."

"Oh, I hope so." Sir Seymour gazed at Harrison as if he'd suddenly turned into a spider or beetle, and Sir Seymour could not anticipate what despicable creature he would transform into next.

"It's not a joke," Harrison said, somewhat perturbed his statement had been met with such shock. No wonder Lucy had never felt at home. Her parents had been brave to try.

"But the United States is filled with those warriors," one man stated. "They slaughtered people. They slaughtered Englishmen. Englishmen whose duty it was simply to protect them."

Harrison furrowed his brow together, suspecting there was something to argue but not certain what exactly.

"Oh yes." Another man nodded his head with equal vigor. "You don't want to go there. Certainly not."

"Well, Boston is perhaps not dreadful," a lone dissenter said.

Sir Seymour narrowed his eyes at this man with rebellious instincts and a contradictory air. "Boston is where the crisis started. None of this devastation would have occurred without Boston."

The man managed to look ashamed and cast his eyes down.

Harrison sighed. It seemed no one else would dare defend Americans in this room now. "Still, they're not so terrible. Some of them are quite nice."

"Nice?" Sir Seymour clutched his heart. "Has that become the criteria all of a sudden? More important than *birth*?"

Harrison had considered these men his friends. He'd discussed which boxer was the best, and whether they'd seen the Beast and the Devil's match at the local boxing ring.

He'd avoided more important issues, and because of that, he realized he did not truly know them.

Blast it, he'd been happy to spend time with them. Perhaps some of them only visited during the day, but he'd thought he'd known all of them.

He certainly hadn't prepared himself for their utter insistence that birth was the most crucial thing in the world. What would they think if they knew his actual identity?

Though his father had been the Duke of Sturbridge, he'd never married Harrison's mother. Harrison was a fraud.

A sour taste invaded his mouth.

"Good God," one man said, "you look as pale as a ghost."

"He's probably practicing to be one," Sir Seymour grumbled. "He'll likely find himself murdered if he goes to that horrible country. That's what happened to my brother."

"And mine," another man murmured.

"I lost my three sons," an elderly man said mournfully.

A few others listed people who had died in the war. Perhaps their prejudice could be explained. Still, Harrison had no urge to remain. "I must pack."

Sir Seymour stared at him with a bewildered expression on his face. "You mean, you must tell your valet to pack."

"Yes."

It was suddenly exceedingly urgent that he leave. Harrison scampered from the room, narrowly tripping over one of the large, Oriental carpets someone had hauled here from Persia or the Ottoman Empire or some other place which was not England.

He rushed up the narrow staircase, away from the bemused expressions of the people he'd once considered his greatest friends. They didn't understand him and never would. His heart clenched, but he forced himself to move.

He couldn't let Lucy think he didn't care about her. If it had been up to him, he would have married her with no question at all. But things were more complicated.

"Would you like me to pack everything?" his valet asked a few minutes later.

"Oh, yes. Thank you, Fletcher."

Fletcher started to put Harrison's stationery away, and it occurred to Harrison he could simply write a letter to Lucy. And yet, this wasn't something one shared in a letter. She might have questions, after all. No, it was far better to take a ship for America. What were some unpleasant waves?

Soon, Fletcher and he entered the carriage, and the astonished driver prepared the horses.

The carriage soon glided regally past the large, immaculate houses in Mayfair. The facades sparkled as always, the white paint immaculately maintained despite the soot and pollution that sometimes stained it. Gradually, the buildings became less lofty, less exquisite. He must be reaching the East End.

The streets were suddenly crowded, but not by barouches and curricles, the common contraptions found in Mayfair and Kensington and the areas he frequented. Rather, actual people were pushing wheelbarrows across the street, leading horses and cows that clomped across the cobblestones. Dirt-stained children stared at him, as if bewildered by the glossiness of his barouche.

It occurred to him that this was where, in truth, he belonged. He hadn't come from money. He'd just become lucky. And now, there was no way to make things right.

Finally, the driver halted the coach at the Port of London. The scent of the Thames was almost overwhelming, and he stared at the murky green and brown water. No wonder Sir Seymour and the other men at the club had been so suspicious of his desire to travel anywhere on it.

Still, he was certain the United States did not deserve all their suspicion and prejudice.

Lucy had not deserved it.

His heart ached, even though he'd relegated any such pain in his chest to a much older future age. Everything was different now.

CHAPTER TWENTY-ONE

The carriage stopped at the Port of London, and Fletcher and Harrison exited. People piled into small boats to take them to the ships docked further away, hauling valises and trunks. Rain drizzled over them, and their faces were determined, no doubt eager not to lose their grasp of their suddenly slippery holdings. The wind swirled more fiercely, as if already prepared to usher the ships away from London.

Thankfully, there was only a small queue in front of the ticket office, and Harrison soon spoke with the ticket master.

"I would like a return ticket to New York," Harrison said.

The gray-haired man nodded. "There's a ship leaving this afternoon."

Harrison's shoulders eased. "That would be perfect."

The man eyed Harrison's clothes. "Would a shared cabin suffice?"

His valet shot a horrified look at the ticket master. "Oh no, this is His Grace, the Duke of Sturbridge. He requires a cabin of his own."

The ticket holder's cheeks pinkened, but he nodded. "Very well. Nothing on this ship, as I said, but there is one at the end of this week, if that would do. We can give you a superb cabin then."

A disgruntled expression came over Fletcher's face, one Harrison had always thought reserved for when Harrison came back to the club with mud on his boots, and his valet lectured him on the importance of boot maintenance.

"The duke intends to go to New York today," Fletcher said.

"Yes, I see." The ticket holder bit his lip. "I am certain I can rearrange some things. Perhaps the captain does not require his captain's suite."

"It will be fine," Harrison interrupted. "Absolutely fine. The important thing is that I get there as soon as possible."

"Are you certain?" Fletcher shot him a quizzical glance. "These ships are already uncomfortable."

The ticket master straightened his body. "I assure you this company works hard to provide a comforting environment for all our passengers."

Fletcher rolled his eyes. "Well, it is still a ship made entirely of wood that sails over waves. I can't think of anything quite as uncomfortable as that."

The ticket master did not argue.

"I can share a room," Harrison said. "It will truly be no problem at all."

"Indeed?" Fletcher shot a worried look at him.

"I am certain I can survive." If Harrison had been a few years older, he would have fought in the Napoleonic Wars. Certainly, a ship could be no comparison to the agony those people experienced.

"You may board," the ticket master said.

"Are you certain, Your Grace?" his valet asked.

"Absolutely, Fletcher. In fact, I'm pleased there's a ship leaving today."

"How stoic of you, Your Grace." Fletcher's eyes sparkled in wonder. "How very admirable." He turned to the ticket master. "Isn't His Grace admirable?"

"Most," the ticket master said cautiously, as if the wrong word might banish him to prison.

Fletcher nodded with a pleased expression, then his face paled. This time, he bit his lip. "Your Grace, do you require my services on your travel? I am, of course, always available for you."

Harrison smiled. "You needn't worry. You can make certain everything is prepared for my return to Cornwall. I would not want you exposed to the hazards of an Atlantic crossing."

Relief flooded Fletcher's face. "Oh, thank you, Your Grace. Thank you so very much."

"You're quite welcome." If Harrison wasn't happy, he was glad he could alleviate Fletcher's worry.

A cloud formed over his valet's face. "Who will choose clothes for you to wear every day?"

"I will manage."

"But the buttons? The cuff links? The sewing?"

"I am aware of how to put on loose buttons," Harrison said.

"Truly?"

Harrison nodded, deciding not to share his skills at sewing and long experience of self-dressing. "Perhaps I will not wear my cuff links for this trip if they prove too complex."

"How very brave of you, Your Grace."

Harrison purchased the ticket. He bade farewell to Fletcher, then headed up the gangway toward the ship. Murky green water tossed the ship back and forth, seagulls swarmed the area, swooping down with the sudden ferocity of cannonballs when they spotted potential food. Harrison forced himself to greet the sailor at the top of the gangway with a smile.

The sailor took his ticket and led him down a steep step of stairs. A musty smell pervaded the narrow dark passage, and Harrison's nostrils flared involuntarily.

The sailor opened the door to a tiny room. Three men played cards. They shot a disappointed look at him, as if they'd hoped his bed would remain empty. Still, they nodded politely.

"Good afternoon." Harrison placed his single trunk on the side.

"Quite fancy clothes you're wearing," one of them remarked.

"Some people take the importance of traveling seriously," the other one said, dealing more cards. He turned to Harrison. "Would you like to play some whist?"

"Oh, no, thank you." Harrison couldn't imagine playing anything now, not when his heart ached. "I'll just lie down."

The other men turned from him, already uninterested in his presence.

Even though it was the middle of the day, and Harrison was not prone to taking naps, he was suddenly very, very tired. The sounds of the men playing cards and exclaiming over their luck and misfortune did not lessen his weariness.

Finally, the ship jerked, and the sounds of sailors shouting drifted through the floorboards. He followed the other men upstairs to watch the ship set sail. Some children clapped their hands in excitement, and even older passengers seemed impressed by the ship's ability to glide along the Thames.

Boats and ships and barges thronged the Thames, and it seemed impossible to think the ship could ever possibly make its way all the way to New York. The ship inched slowly through the barrage of traffic.

Harrison lingered above the deck. London's grimy buildings receded in size until the only thing he could see were large swathes of flat land unmarred by any mountains. What had Lucy made of the scenery when she'd sailed a few days before?

If only Lucy were here, so he might speak with her. He'd enjoyed every moment with her, even the ones he complained about.

Heavens, he missed *her*. He missed her so very much. No doubt, he always would.

HOME.

Lucy said the word in her mind and tried to conjure the requisite joy as the carriage rumbled over the cobblestones toward her parents' Fifth Avenue house. She'd long since stopped crying, and her parents avoided the subject of Harrison, as if he had never existed.

When the familiar buildings swirled past and her family's servants greeted them with enjoyment, Lucy's smile was not forced. The house sparkled in its customary manner, and sunbeams gleamed over the polished wooden floorboards.

Lucy ascended the steps to her bedroom, and Lucy's maid, Eliza, soon entered the room with Lucy's bags.

"Did you have a good time in London?" Eliza's wide smile exceeded even that of her normal enthusiasm.

Lucy hesitated, then simply nodded. Eliza didn't want to hear a negative story that involved her heart aching. Besides, most of it *had* been good. Except the end. That, certainly, had been dreadful.

"Oh, I am so envious of you. It must've been so wonderful." Eliza chatted happily as she unpacked Lucy's trunks, putting some clothes aside to take down to the kitchen to work on later. "How incredible you were there."

"Yes." Lucy smiled. She'd forgotten that that had been incredible.

"Was it every bit as wonderful as you thought? You must tell me everything."

"It was wonderful," Lucy agreed.

Eliza's eyes shimmered. "Did you meet any lords?"

"There were a great many."

Now, Eliza's eyes both shimmered and widened. "Indeed? Earls?"

"Yes. And some viscounts, marquesses, and also some dukes."

"Dukes." Eliza sighed. She held her hand over her heart as she gazed at Lucy in wonder. She plopped onto Lucy's bed before she hastily bounced up. "I'm sorry, miss. I don't usually sit here."

"You were taken aback."

"Most certainly." Eliza nodded hastily, and her white cap slid down with the force of her movement. She tucked it back into place. "How incredible. I must ask Rose all about your trip."

"I'm sure she has some stories to tell."

"Oh, I imagine. Did you go to any balls?"

"Yes."

"Just like Cinderella. Oh my."

"There are balls in New York for me to go to."

"Oh, but they can't be the same. They can't compare." Eliza shook her head with a firmness she normally devoted to ascribing the unpleasantness of beholding a poorly creased dress.

Lucy strode to her bay window. The view might not be of Grosvenor Square, but it remained good. It was home, and that was enough.

In time she might even forget Harrison. Somehow, the thought did not seem reassuring. Still, she gazed out the window. Other buildings stared at her, and she reminded herself not to miss Grosvenor Square's leafy trees.

CHAPTER TWENTY-TWO

Traveling on a ship over the Atlantic was every bit as horrendous as Fletcher had indicated. Harrison lay tightly against the top berth. Even turning to the side was apparently a luxury. Now, it was all but impossible.

This was the life the duchess had warned him against. This was the life that was truly his.

Rain splattered over the ship with great frequency, and even when it did not, waves were bound to fling salty spray over the deck, as if astounded that any manmade construction would ever think of breaching its borders. There'd been only a single night, early on the journey, that he'd crept up to the deck to sleep underneath the stars with the other men in less than desirable accommodation.

Today was different from the other days. Today they were supposed to land in New York.

The other men in the cabin smiled with excitement, but nervousness thrummed through Harrison.

Finally, sailors shouted that New York was visible, and Harrison followed the others to the deck. Passengers filled the area, their heads turned to one direction: New York City. As they approached, Harrison stared as well.

"It's incredible," one person murmured.

The ship's sailors shouted as they moved in a choreographed manner, taking down the sails and tossing ropes.

Finally, the ship anchored, and shore boats approached.

Most people lugged large pieces of luggage onto the shore boats. Clearly, most of them had no intention of ever returning to England. What might that be like? To be able to change one's life so completely?

"How long do you plan to stay?" one of the men asked him.

"Hopefully, I can return on this ship."

The person blinked. "You don't intend to see anything when you're here?"

"I plan to have a conversation with someone here, but I doubt that will take long."

The man stared at him, obviously baffled. "My word."

"Some conversations are simply more proper to have in person."

"I suppose that's correct," another man said, but his eyes still narrowed, as if half suspecting Harrison was displaying signs of madness.

NOISES SOUNDED FROM downstairs, and Lucy furrowed her brow, removing her gaze from her book reluctantly.

Still, the noises continued, even though Lucy was certain nobody had planned a gathering at this time.

It was six on a Tuesday evening, hardly the time for callers.

"Lucy? Lucy?" Footsteps pounded toward her, then Eliza dashed into the room. "Miss Banks. Oh, you must come."

Lucy snapped her book shut. "Is there something wrong?"

Eliza shook her head. "You have a guest."

Lucy blinked.

"So not very wrong at all," Eliza added uncertainly.

Evidently, even the servants thought she was an unsocial being if having a guest caused such surprise. "Who is it? Is it Beatrice? Or perhaps Bessie? Patricia?"

"Oh no, miss. It's a most handsome gentleman."

"Indeed?" Lucy sighed. "Are you certain it's for me? It might be for Isabella. Normally, handsome men call on Isabella. Of course, she's not here, but he might not know that."

"Oh no, miss. He specifically asked for you."

"Well, he could have gotten my name wrong." Lucy opened her book again. "That's probably the case. Did my parents tell you to find me?"

Eliza's apple cheeks suddenly pinkened. "No." She tugged on her apron. "I'm—er—afraid I overheard when I was cleaning one of the rooms on the corridor. In fact, they—er—told him to leave."

"Then this is somebody they don't want me to see."

"He did seem most insistent, miss."

Something occurred to Lucy. Something that made her heart spin. But she put away the thought quickly and scolded her hands for fluttering. Obviously, it could not be *him*. No, *he* lived in London and sometimes in Cornwall. He certainly never ever came here.

Obviously, this visitor's appearance simply reminded her of him. It would be absurd to think *he* was here. There was nothing to muse upon at all.

"I'm certain there must have been some misunderstanding," she said.

"You're not curious, miss? He has the most wonderful English accent. It was most amazing." Eliza's long eyelashes beat up and down, as if they were even now incredulous that they'd seen such a glorious compilation of masculinity.

Heavens.

"I suppose I am curious." Lucy put down her book and crept from the room.

And there *he* was, standing in the corridor.

Harrison.

Lucy's heart squeezed and soared. "You're here."

"Yes," Harrison said, and he gazed at her with such fondness that her heart lurched even further, intent on finding a higher perch.

Unfortunately, Mama and Papa were also in the corridor.

"You mustn't talk to him," Mama said.

"Yes," Papa agreed, a rare occasion for both of them.

Mama scowled and marched toward her. She pushed her back into her bedroom.

Lucy hurried back to the hallway.

"I'm going to throw you out, young man," Papa told Harrison.

"Are you strong enough for that?" Mama asked.

"Well, we are on the second floor, my dear. Now, if I simply start charging at him while that window is open, there is a chance that through mere physics . . . "

Lucy swallowed hard, and her gaze followed Papa's to an open window.

An image of Harrison flying to the ground assaulted her mind. "That's enough, Papa."

Harrison glanced uncertainly at the window as if he were also wondering whether it would be better to lock it now as a precautionary measure.

"I'll speak with him," Lucy said.

Mama narrowed her eyes. "Absolutely not."

Papa crossed his arms and glared at Harrison. "Have you come to propose to my daughter?"

The air thickened, and Lucy's heart quickened. Had he come to propose? Was that why he was here? Men didn't generally travel on four-week journeys.

Harrison's face pinkened, and he shook his head. "No, I haven't."

Lucy's heart tumbled, but it didn't matter. She'd known that anyway. She firmed her lips and made certain her chin didn't wobble. Harrison was not going to see her unhappy. Nobody was.

"You mustn't ask him these questions, Papa," Lucy said.

"It is my duty, dear child," her father replied, "to ensure you are not alone with this man. Perhaps one day you'll have children of your own and will understand."

"Oh, that's very doubtful," Mama said. "Very doubtful, indeed."

Eliza's mouth dropped, and Lucy's heart sank even further.

This was the sort of thing people would gossip about. What didn't her parents understand? They weren't making anything better. They were just making everything worse. If they wanted to protect her, this was not the way to do it.

And if Harrison had traveled all the way across the Atlantic just to speak with her, well, she could listen to him, couldn't she?

Lucy placed her arms on her waist. "You're not being helpful. You're never helpful."

"That's nonsense."

"You took me all the way to Europe, but it didn't help."

Mama's face paled.

"I was happy in New York. I didn't need to be hauled to Europe. That didn't improve my life. That wasn't what I wanted."

"I won't tolerate any more of this ingratitude, Lucy." Mama clutched her heart. "It's simply too horrific to imagine. After everything we've done for you."

"The point is, Mother, that perhaps you don't know best."

Mama's face paled, and for once, she was silent. In the next moment, Mama's eyelashes started to furiously blink, and nausea crept up Lucy's throat.

She'd said too much.

"I am sorry, Mother. I-I was difficult. I *am* difficult. Isabella is betrothed, after all."

Mama nodded, obviously happy by that thought.

Lucy's throat dried. She'd never be able to give Mama that same happiness.

"I shouldn't have come here. I'll leave now." Harrison bowed to Papa, Mama, and then finally to Lucy. His eyes were sorrowful, then he swung around and strolled from the room.

"Well." Mama sighed and plopped onto Lucy's bed. "That was shocking."

"Most shocking." Papa still stared at the open door.

"To think he came all the way here," Mama said.

"Yes. Most odd. That's man is up to no good. I'm certain," Papa nodded gravely with the same somberness with which he chose stocks.

Lucy wanted to argue with them, but instead, she strode from the room and glanced at her parents. They were still remarking over their shock.

Lucy descended the staircase, brushed past the startled butler and dashed outside. She wasn't certain how many minutes she had.

"Harrison, Harrison!" she called.

He swung around and smiled when he saw her. "You came."

"I thought it might be important, given the whole traveling across the ocean thing."

"Very astute." His eyes took on a tender quality. "Would you care to join me for a stroll?"

CHAPTER TWENTY-THREE

Lucy Banks was here beside him, and Harrison's heart warmed. She looked marvelous. Her red hair gleamed against her emerald afternoon dress. He wanted to kiss every freckle. He wanted to kiss her.

Her large eyes looked at him questioningly, and he remembered he was supposed to speak. His throat dried. There was so much he needed to tell her, but all he wanted to do was take her in his arms.

He didn't want to think about what her reaction to his secret to be.

Carriages rolled by, and they proceeded to stroll along Fifth Avenue. Well-dressed men and women passed them, speaking in the same accent as Lucy.

"How do you like New York?" Lucy asked.

"So far, I've only seen the harbor and here."

"I see."

"But it was quite nice."

"Oh, good. I'm glad." She gave him her customary wide smile.

"Everyone is friendly." Then he paused and frowned.

Her succulent lips twitched, as if arguing whether to laugh at his expression. "You mean everyone is friendly except for my parents?"

He nodded. "Yes, that is more correct." Then he shot a guilty look at her. "I mean, normally your parents are nice and friendly. That was my first impression of them. It's just that—"

"Things have changed," Lucy finished for him, and her face sobered.

"Yes. That's my fault. I'm sorry I landed you in this. I hurt you."

She gave him a wobbly smile that managed to strike him in the chest. Polo balls had less force.

Damnation.

He didn't want her unhappiness, and he certainly didn't want her to mask her emotions. She should be pummeling him with her fists.

Harrison put his hands around hers, and energy surged through him. Lucy had left the house so quickly she hadn't taken her gloves, and every curve of her slender hands was apparent. They were small against his own. "I'm so sorry."

Lucy averted her gaze, but he needed to continue. She had to know.

"I never wanted to involve you in my past," Harrison said. "I never wanted to involve you in my secrets. I love you. I love you completely and utterly."

The air was suddenly still, even though he was certain he should be hearing the cacophony of conversation, trotting of horses, and rumbling of carriage wheels over the tilestones.

Lucy's mouth opened. "And I—"

He pressed his finger to her lips and pretended he didn't want to taste them. "Nothing has changed, of course. You needn't say anything."

She frowned slightly. "If you truly do love—"

"I do," he said quickly. "I wouldn't say it otherwise."

Confusion flitted over her face. "Why cannot you marry me?"

"Right." He inhaled, then exhaled. Then inhaled and exhaled again. Normally, Harrison didn't have such trouble talking, and she tilted her head. Concern filled her eyes.

Lucy looked down and fiddled with her sleeves. "I'm sorry. You don't have to tell me. I suppose you want to marry someone British, someone with a title. Someone who can be a true Duchess of Sturbridge. Someone not like me. I-I understand."

"No. That's not the reason. I have to tell you the whole story. It began when I was born."

She stifled a laugh. "That sounds like it could be a very long story."

"In fact, it started before I was born. My father, you see, is the Duke of Sturbridge."

"Yes."

"But I don't think you know who my mother is."

She furrowed her brow. "I've met your mother."

"You've met the Duchess of Sturbridge."

"I don't understand," Lucy said, but she looked like she was beginning to do so.

"My mother was a parlor maid at the house."

Lucy turned and stared at him. "But that's not . . . I don't understand. It's not possible."

"My father enjoyed spending time with women. It's an activity I've also found pleasurable."

Lucy averted her gaze.

"Not that that's of importance," the duke said hastily. "But the point is, my father had a son with his wife, and then at nearly the same time, he had a son with the scullery maid."

"I don't understand. You're a duke, and well—"

He gave a wry smile. "Dukes don't have mothers who were scullery maids. They certainly don't have mothers who weren't married to their fathers. My brother—half-brother—was never well. We were tutored together. I'm not certain the duchess even knew I was the duke's son to begin with, though I think by the time I was two, it would have been fairly obvious, judging by the portraits. I have this." He brushed a finger against his sturdy jaw, then pointed at his Roman nose. "And I have this."

"I see," Lucy said faintly.

"My father died, then my brother."

"I'm so sorry."

Harrison shrugged. "We weren't particularly close. But since we were the same age, we spent all our time together. It's common for aristocrats to have tutors teach their children, along with servants' children. It's not a horrible thing for servants' children to have some education. Maybe they hoped I could be more helpful on the estate once I learned to read. It's also not a horrible thing for aristocrats' children to have some added stimulus in the classroom. My brother was always sickly. They always worried he would die. He didn't go to boarding school because of his health. And then both the duke and he died. Tuberculosis."

"How dreadful to lose them both."

"I was even less close to my father. I was an embarrassment."

"What happened?" Lucy asked.

"Rightfully, my education should have stopped. I should have simply become a servant, perhaps a valet or butler, because of my education. That's what would have been customary."

"But that's not what happened."

"No. The duchess liked me. I reminded her of her late husband. You see? And I reminded her of her son, who was dead. I suppose she could have hated me, but she didn't. She was a nice woman. She *is* a nice woman. She was also concerned about what would happen to her. She didn't want to leave the castle so some distant relation of her late husband could barge in. And she felt that . . ."

"Oh." Lucy blinked. No doubt, she knew where this was going.

"I think you understand. Since so few people had actually met my brother, she thought she could simply declare me the new duke."

"I see."

"She could keep me at home, continue my education, obviously with a new tutor. And the few servants there who knew what had occurred would be silent, conscious that if they weren't, some stranger would come to the castle with his own servants and disrupt their lives."

"They must have liked you. They could have resented you."

"Yes. I was lucky, I suppose. They liked me."

"And you went along with it?"

"I was twelve. I was being offered the chance to be a duke by a woman who had provided everything for me. I didn't like seeing her distraught. And I'm afraid since my father had been the duke, I thought maybe it wouldn't be truly wrong to pretend to be one."

"So your true name is not Harrison?"

"No." Harrison smiled, and his eyes adopted a dewy quality as if he were witnessing a far-off memory. "It's Samuel actually, though I haven't heard that name in a while. You can call me Harrison."

"Very well."

"But only afterward did I realize this was a game I could not renounce. Changing my mind is an impossibility. The law might not look kindly on someone who impersonated a duke for years. If someone discovers my deception, I would destroy my life and that of my family. So, you see, I can never marry. I can never let any woman, no matter how much they cared for me, no matter how much I cared for her, risk ruining her life."

She stared at him. "Go on."

"I can't marry knowing any children we were to have might be suddenly, violently disinherited. It wouldn't be right."

"You should have told me," Lucy said.

"I-I wanted to do so," Harrison said. "In the boat, on the Serpentine, I almost did. I-I hated myself for being so weak. I-I hated myself for the secret too."

Lucy bit her lip.

"I'm sorry," Harrison said. "That's what I came to tell you. I should have been better at staying away from you. And I certainly shouldn't have kissed you."

"I thought you didn't want to marry me because I wasn't duchess material."

He gave a sad smile. "I assure you, Lucy Banks, that you would be an excellent duchess. Unfortunately, I'm not just a faux suitor. I'm also a faux duke."

"I'm sorry I asked you to pretend," Lucy said softly.

"I'm not sorry," he said. "I-I enjoyed myself. Too much."

"That must have been a difficult secret to bear," Lucy said.

"I've felt guilty my whole life," Harrison confessed. "I'm not leading the life I should lead. I should be in service. I shouldn't be the person being served."

"You were being helpful," Lucy said.

Harrison gave a wry smile. "It's what a good servant does, isn't it? You're rich and beautiful and intelligent. You don't need a life with me. My life could be destroyed at any moment. I don't want you to have that scandal, I don't want any children to bear that scandal. I don't even want your family to be affected by that scandal."

Lucy nodded.

"I trust you'll keep it secret?"

"Of course, I will."

"I wouldn't blame you if you told everyone."

"I won't. I would never do that to you."

"I thought you wouldn't." He sighed. "I should go. It's a long way back to London."

She nodded, but he continued to stare at her. He cupped her cheek with his hand, and a rush of heat moved through him at the contact. "Farewell, dear Lucy."

HARRISON HAD JUST SAID goodbye to her. This was when she was supposed to turn around and return to her home.

Instead, she hesitated. Her heart ached, imagining that twelve-year-old boy who'd had his whole life changed at the request of his grieving employer. Everything now made sense.

"You have another option," Lucy blurted.

Harrison wrinkled his brow. "What do you mean?"

"You *could* renounce your dukedom. I'm not saying it for my sake, of course," she continued hastily. "I don't want you to think that. But if the dukedom is a burden to you, you do not have to keep it."

"But Parliament—"

"I know. But you were a child when it started. They might be lenient."

Harrison shook his head. "They would be betrayed. And they would want to make certain no one else attempts a similar deception."

"Move here." Lucy grasped hold of his hand. "This is a whole country where people don't care about your past."

He blinked.

"I mean, they might find your past mysterious and intriguing, but I don't think you would experience the same snobbery as you would in England. You would not worry about the law."

Perhaps he had no interest in such a life. He was a duke, after all. Or at least, he lived like one.

Her cheeks warmed, and she ducked her head. "I'm sorry. It was probably a silly idea. I understand you don't want to do anything. And I do respect that. I do. He was your father, after all. You *are* the son of a duke."

Harrison shook his head. "I think it's not actually such a terrible idea."

"Well, I make a point of not giving out terrible ideas. Only potentially mediocre ones." She laughed weakly, but her voice struggled against her ever-tightening diaphragm.

"Not mediocre."

Her lips tightened into a polite smile. "I should return now. My parents might notice I'm gone, and I would hardly want to bring them out screaming on the street especially—"

"Since this might be my new home," he murmured, his tone silky.

This time she stared.

"You mean to move here?" Her voice was soft.

He nodded solemnly. "I have one condition, though."

"Is it something I can help with?"

"Yes," he said. "You would be essential to it. Most essential."

"Well, if I can help," she said uncertainly, unsure how she could be the least bit useful.

For some reason, his eyes glimmered. "My question is this: would you do me the great, utmost highest honor of becoming my wife?"

Lucy's mouth dropped open. She must have misheard him. She tucked some hair behind her ear as if the action might help her hear better. "I don't understand."

"It's a proposal."

She stared up at him. He couldn't mean that.

"It's a marriage proposal." He took her hands in his, and her heartbeat quickened. He was gazing at her with such intensity. "I would like you, Lucy Banks, to be my wife."

"You don't mean that."

"I absolutely do."

"No." She shook her head. "You would be escaping the life you liked. It was a silly suggestion. I never should've made it."

"I love you, Lucy," he said, and his voice was calm. "It was the hardest thing to not propose to you all year. And when I discovered you had gone to New York, and I would never see you again..."

"That's why you followed me?"

"I didn't want you to think my hesitance to marry had anything to do with you. I didn't want to put you in a difficult position. I didn't want our children to be in a difficult position."

"Did you just say our children?" Her voice shook.

"Oh yes, Lucy, our children. Let's have many. What do you say, my dear?"

Heavens.

This was truly happening. He loved her and wanted to marry her.

She nodded hastily, and he grinned and took her in his arms. His sturdy muscular arms pressed against her waist. In the next moment, he was kissing her and kissing her and kissing her.

Finally, he withdrew his arms from her reluctantly. "I think perhaps we should tell your parents. If you'll still have me."

"Oh, I will," she said. "I most certainly will."

They marched back to the townhouse, striding side by side. Their fingers touched, then their hands clutched together as they began their new life.

CHAPTER TWENTY-FOUR

Harrison's shoulders eased, and the tightness that had encircled his heart alleviated. Lucy was here beside him. She was going to marry him, and he wasn't going to lie anymore.

There would be no more deception.

The duchess would be upset of course. She'd have to make do with the amount the late duke had given to her in his will. Unless they were able to trace some far-flung relative, the dukedom would revert to the crown. Harrison wouldn't be surprised if the duchess tried to petition Parliament itself to let her maintain her position. He gave a wry smile.

But it was for the best. It would be what should have happened long ago.

This would be his new home. He looked around, noting the bustling carriages, the elegant mansions built by people who'd made something of themselves. Lucy's father had been poor when he'd arrived in New York. He hadn't spent his time gambling, like so many of the *ton,* eager to alleviate their boredom by whatever means possible. Anything here was possible.

Excitement thrummed through Harrison. Perhaps he would never be able to return to England without fear of the law, but perhaps that didn't matter. He didn't care what people like Sir Seymour thought.

The sun glinted against Lucy's magnificent red hair and cast a golden glow about her sumptuous body. He forced himself to not simply barrage her with compliments. He loved her. He loved her so much. It had been difficult for him to go against his instincts for so long, but now he could tell her. He never wanted to stop telling her.

Lucy and he ascended the short flight of steps and reentered the house. The butler swallowed hard, and his eyes flickered to Harrison's and Lucy's enjoined hands. He drew back. "Great Scott!" The butler's cheeks reddened. "I'm sorry."

"It's fine," Lucy said reassuringly. She beamed. "In fact, everything's fine."

They exchanged a glance, and Harrison's heart warmed even more.

"What's all this?" Mr. Banks's voice boomed from the top of the stairs, then he stomped down. "It's you again." He fixed a hard stare on Harrison. "I told you to go away."

"Look," Mrs. Banks interrupted, and she pointed at Harrison's hand. More specifically, Harrison's fingers, which were entwined with Lucy's. "They're holding hands."

Mr. Banks's frown turned deeper and more ferocious. "What are you doing?" He glanced at the butler. "Reynolds, bring me a gun."

Lucy shot a nervous look at Harrison as if she half expected him to let go and sprint all the way to the very first ship back to England.

Harrison wasn't going to do that. He loved Lucy and would marry her.

"I have an announcement to make," Harrison said.

"That you're an idiot?" Mr. Banks asked.

"No."

"That you are a scoundrel?" Mr. Banks suggested, and his eyes narrowed.

"No."

"Perhaps we should hear what he has to say." Mrs. Banks still stared at his and Lucy's hands.

"We are going to marry," Harrison said.

Mrs. Banks clapped her hands. "My son-in-law is to be a duke. My daughter will be a duchess. This is the pinnacle of my happiness."

"Well, actually . . ." Harrison said. "There's something you should probably know."

"I know you should be inside this house talking instead of outside of it." Mrs. Banks ushered them both inside and shot a stern look at her husband. "You shouldn't have frightened him so much. Most likely, he would have proposed long ago if you hadn't been so terrifying."

"Terrifying, you say?" Mr. Banks's eyes twinkled.

"It was not meant to be a compliment," Mrs. Banks said.

"I'll take it as one." Mr. Banks slapped Harrison on his back with such force that Harrison nearly fell to the floor, even though he was in no manner weak.

"You're going to be my son-in-law," Mr. Banks said jovially, and all the scowls and glowers were gone. "Welcome to the family."

In the next moment, he tackled Harrison in a large hug.

Harrison blinked. "Mr. Banks?"

"You can call me Papa now," Mr. Banks said.

"Papa?" Harrison tested.

"Yes, exactly. Two syllables."

"Papa," Harrison said.

Mr. Banks grinned and jerked his thumb at Lucy. "It took us eight months to teach you that word. And this man, this fellow, it just took him two seconds to learn. He'll be quite a husband for you."

"HE'S RENOUNCING HIS dukedom, Mama," Lucy said.

"Well, renouncing is not quite the right word." Harrison looked at Lucy.

"I know," she whispered. "But one thing at a time."

"Wait. You're not going to be a duke?" Mrs. Banks' eyebrows rose.

"No," Harrison replied.

"Oh, no! Well, what do you say, Mr. Banks, about that? How horrible. How tricky. How . . ."

"Well, I don't see anything wrong with that at all," Mr. Banks said. "I thought all that title business was nonsense."

"You're not supposed to say that." His wife elbowed him.

"I only speak the truth." He grinned. "We're elated to have you join us."

"But, darling. Maybe we should reconsider if he's not a duke."

"No. He is marrying our Lucy."

"But you despised him before," Mrs. Banks wailed. "Why can't you do so again? Why must you always be so disagreeable?"

"I'm sorry," Mr. Banks told Harrison. "She'll calm down eventually."

"Or find something else to worry about," Harrison suggested.

"Yes, that's possible. Sometimes that's the only solution." Mr. Banks glanced at his wife. "Both your daughters are getting married."

"I'll be alone." Mrs. Banks continued to cry. "Both my children gone, departed from the house."

Mr. Banks nodded at Harrison. "See, it worked."

Harrison wasn't certain this was an improvement on his wife's previous state, and he had the odd suspicion Mr. Banks didn't quite care either way.

He sighed. Still, he had Lucy in his life, and that was the important thing. Even if sometimes her parents were difficult.

"Well, Mama. You needn't worry," Lucy said. "We plan to move here, to New York."

"Oh, my baby." Mrs. Banks dashed toward Lucy and embraced her into a hug. "You'll be here." She turned to Harrison. "Is this really true?"

"That's our plan," Harrison said.

"Well, it's a good plan."

"I will need work, though," Harrison said.

"Heavens, you are becoming American."

Harrison grinned. "That's not a bad thing to be."

Mr. Banks slapped him on the back. "I'll take you round to my office tomorrow. My wife already tells me I'm far too busy. It will be nice to have some help. I'll teach you everything I know, then we'll get you voted in to join the New York Stock and Exchange Board." Mr. Banks gave a smug grin. "I know a lot."

Harrison turned to Lucy. He'd thought he would never see her again, and then he'd thought he'd only see her to have one brief awkward conversation. He hadn't thought he might marry her, that there might be a way that he could find happiness.

His heart filled with images of what might happen in the future. Places they might go. Balls they might dance at. Picnics they could have and children, laughing and dancing, that they would make.

"I'm the luckiest man in the world." Harrison turned to Lucy, and even though her parents were nearby, he dipped her into a long kiss and kissed and kissed and kissed.

"Oh my," Mrs. Banks exclaimed.

When they stood up, Mrs. Banks stared at him, her hand on her heart.

Lucy's eyes glimmered. "I'm quite a lucky woman too."

EPILOGUE

Several Months Later

"Isabella and Lord Brooke are inside," Mama announced. "The place is quite full."

Normally, Lucy might have given a nervous giggle like she would have done in London, but instead, Lucy merely smiled. "Oh, good. That means we can start soon."

"Let's practice one more time." Mama grabbed Papa's arm and practiced striding down the aisle.

"I know how to walk," Papa grumbled.

"Yes, but this is walking on an aisle when everyone sees you. It's different. It has to be in rhythm to the music," Mama explained.

Papa grunted. "It's not difficult. I taught Lucy and Isabella how to walk. Most people leave it to the nannies, but no, I taught them myself."

"You just waved to them from their nursery from time to time," Mama said.

"And they came walking to me," Papa said proudly.

"They were always too fond of you," Mama griped, but she didn't seem incredibly upset. "Still, we need to practice it."

She started humming the wedding march song. "Now, at this beat, you lift your leg this way, and at that beat, lift your other leg that way."

"It's just walking," Papa said.

"Not just walking," Mama insisted. "Explain, Lucy."

"I'm sure you'll be good at it," Lucy said smoothly.

"Ha," Papa said with pride. "She can see that I've mastered the art long ago."

"Well, she can certainly see your gray hair, that's for sure," Mama said. "There's still time to put some shoe polish on it."

Papa shuddered.

"When the portraitist comes, don't complain to me that your hair is gray."

"You're getting a portrait done?" Eliza asked, as she lifted a mirror to the back of Lucy's head so she could examine her hair from that angle.

Lucy nodded. "This is something we always want to remember. Besides, I want a portrait of my family at the new townhouse."

"How nice."

"Yes," Lucy agreed, "it is."

"The wedding is beginning soon." Mama fluttered around and waved her hands as if it was her personal duty to ensure each and every flower was perfectly adjusted.

"It's happening!" she cried. "Can you believe it, Mr. Banks?"

"I would hope it was happening, considering the amount of visits Harrison has been making to our townhouse."

Mama rushed toward her. "Are your stays tight enough?"

"Yes," Lucy said firmly. "They don't need to be any tighter than this."

Mama scrunched her lips together, as if wondering whether she should suggest that Eliza put a foot against Lucy's back to tighten them a tiny bit further.

Lucy glanced at Eliza. "I think we should hurry."

Eliza nodded and helped Lucy up. She nearly toppled under the weight of her gown. Perhaps Harrison no longer had money, but her parents still did.

"Oh, that looks lovely, dear!" Mama exclaimed.

"I hope so." Lucy stared at the massive swath of fabric.

Was there any chance that the seamstress had managed to make something three times too large? All this fabric didn't seem necessary, but after Eliza continued to assist her, it looked nicer and nicer until finally Mama exclaimed and clapped her hands.

"Oh, my dearest darling. You look beautiful! Ever so beautiful." A wide smile burst onto her face, and her eyes sparkled. "Perhaps we could do something about your freckles. Perhaps some lemon juice now?"

"There's no time to start trying to hide my freckles," Lucy said. "Besides, I don't think Harrison minds them. In fact, he said he's quite fond of them."

Eliza smoothed the dress, so there were no wrinkles, then she fluffed the puff sleeves.

"Very stunning, my dear," Papa said.

Lucy took her father's arm, and they exited the dressing room. The organist spotted them and smiled. They waited as the organist sat down and started to play.

Mama had ensured that huge vases filled with flowers adorned the aisles, and long, generously sized garlands swung from other portions of the church. She inhaled the floral scent, closing her eyes. This was spectacular.

Rows of immaculately dressed women and men, sporting patterns she recognized from the top fashion houses in Paris, stared. They wore large hats adorned with flowers and feathers and fruit.

"Last chance to change your mind," Papa said, as Mama hurried down the aisle to watch from the front.

Lucy giggled. "That will never happen."

"Good. I'm quite fond of him too."

"I know."

The music played, and they walked elegantly, if not always precisely, down the aisle. Harrison faced the altar, as he was supposed to, and she stared at his strong and sturdy back. Her heart warmed.

Mama beamed as they strode nearer. She did not appear the least bit critical of Papa's strides or the fact he walked down the aisle with perhaps more speed than was necessary.

She reached Harrison, and his delicious cotton and citrus scent wafted over her. Happiness emanated through Lucy.

He tilted his head toward her.

"Are you ready for your new life?" she asked.

He grinned. "Absolutely."

MEET THE AUTHOR

Born in Texas, Bianca Blythe spent four years in England. She worked in a fifteenth-century castle, though sadly that didn't actually involve spotting dukes and earls strutting about in Hessians.

She credits British weather for forcing her into a library, where she discovered her first Julia Quinn novel. Thank goodness for blustery downpours.

Bianca now lives in California with her husband.